NIGHT OF THE LIVING TED

NIGHT OF THE LIVING TED

BARRY HUTCHISON ILLUSTRATED BY LEE COSGROVE

Delacorte Press

Text copyright © 2020 by Barry Hutchison
Cover art copyright © 2020 by Lee Cosgrove

All rights reserved. Published in the United States by Delacorte Press,
an imprint of Random House Children's Books, a division of
Penguin Random House LLC, New York.
Originally published in hardcover in the UK by
Stripes Publishing, an imprint of the Little Tiger Group, in 2018.

Delacorte Press and the colophon are registered trademarks of
Penguin Random House LLC.

Visit us on the Web! rhcbooks.com
Educators and librarians, for a variety of teaching tools,
visit us at RHTeachersLibrarians.com

Library of Congress Cataloging-in-Publication Data is available upon request.
ISBN 978-0-593-17428-9 (HC) — ISBN 978-0-593-17429-6 (ebook)

Printed in the United States of America
10 9 8 7 6 5 4 3 2 1

For the teachers and pupils, past and present,
at Wexford Educate Together school
—B.H.

For Cara and Finn,
World Ketchup-Eating Champions
&
Katie—Head Ketchup Wiper
—L.C.

"I mean . . . seriously. Money. Actual money."

Lisa Marie breathed out and watched her breath form clouds of condensation in the air. She'd been doing the same thing for the whole walk into town. It was either that or listen to her big brother's incessant moaning.

She liked that word. *Incessant.* It meant "going on and on and on." Big words were one of Lisa Marie's favorite things, along with science, reading and chip-shop curry sauce (although not necessarily in that order).

Vernon had only been her big brother for a year, but Lisa Marie had already worked out that his favorite things were complaining, moaning and whining. Again, not necessarily in that order.

"I don't see why I've got to buy him a birthday present," Vernon grumbled. "He's not *my* dad."

Lisa Marie wheezed out another cloud of white vapor. *It's not fair,* she silently mouthed.

"It's not fair!"

"Well . . . ," Lisa Marie began, but Vernon was still mid-rant.

"I mean, he's all right, I like him and everything, but why do I have to use my own money to buy him a present?"

"You aren't using your own money," Lisa Marie pointed out. "Mom gave you twenty dollars."

"Exactly. She *gave* it to me, so now it's mine," Vernon said. "I mean, that's just science, or whatever."

Lisa Marie decided not to bother pointing out that (A) no, that wasn't science, actually, and (B) Mom had given him the money *specifically* so he could buy his stepdad a present. Arguing with Vernon was like trying to reason with a plank of wood.

Instead, she went back to breathing vapor clouds and looking in the windows of all the shops they walked past.

Tonight was Halloween, and almost every shop was decorated with black, orange and green displays. Some of them had fake cobwebs covering their shelves, or plastic bats dangling from elastic at the top of the windows.

"What about that?" Vernon asked, pointing at one of the windows. A flimsy plastic skeleton hung from a hook, its arms limp by its sides. "I bet he'd love that."

Lisa Marie frowned. To the best of her knowledge, Dad had never displayed any interest in skeletons, plastic or otherwise. It was only when she saw the price tag that her stepbrother's suggestion made sense.

"And you're not just saying that because it's ninety-nine cents?" she asked.

"Is it?" Vernon asked, trying to sound surprised. "I hadn't even noticed. That's a bonus, isn't it?"

Vernon's mom had offered Lisa Marie the same amount of money she'd given Vernon, but Lisa Marie had wanted to use her own. It felt like the gift would mean more that way.

"Wait! Be quiet!" Vernon hissed.

"I wasn't saying anything," Lisa Marie pointed out, but Vernon had spotted something up ahead and broken into a run, leaving her talking to herself.

She caught up with him outside her favorite shop. Create-a-Ted was a store that let you make your own teddy bears, dress them and take them home. Lisa Marie had built up quite a collection over the years, all in different costumes. The Arctic Explorer bear was her favorite, and took pride of place on the shelf above her bed.

She was surprised to see Vernon standing looking in the window, because he usually hurried past the place making heaving noises like he was throwing up.

There were two signs in the window. One of them was small and a bit upsetting.

It read: UNDER NEW OWNERSHIP.

Lisa Marie had always liked Mr. and Mrs. Chang, the shop's owners. They were a friendly old couple who sometimes let her use the stuffing machine herself. She wished she'd known they were leaving. She'd have made them a Good Luck card.

The other sign was much larger, and was still in the process of being pasted onto the inside of the glass.

FREE HALLOWEEN BEAR—TODAY ONLY!

"Look. *Free!*" Vernon said. "That's even better than ninety-nine cents!"

"I know!" Lisa Marie said. She frowned. "Wait, what are you saying?"

"Your dad's birthday. I can get him a free bear. Boom. Job done. Mom said I could keep the change." He grinned. "So twenty bucks minus one free bear is . . ."

There was a moment of silence. Lisa Marie sighed.

"Twenty bucks."

"Right. Exactly!" Vernon said.

"You want to get a forty-two-year-old man a teddy bear for his birthday?" Lisa Marie asked.

"Yes! Who doesn't love teddy bears?" Vernon said. "Except me, obviously. I think they're stupid. Bleurgh! But your dad will *love* one."

On the other side of the glass, a youngish-looking man with thick-rimmed glasses leaned out from behind the sign. He jumped in fright when he spotted the two children staring at him, then smiled and beckoned them in.

Vernon raced inside, sending the bell above the door into a frenzy of *ding-a-ling-ling*s. Lisa Marie followed and immediately let out a gasp of shock. The shop had completely changed inside, and not for the better.

All the colorful displays of fully stuffed bears had been shoved into one corner. A tarpaulin had been draped in front of the Costumes & Accessories section, hiding all the adorable little bear outfits.

A large cardboard box had been dumped in the middle of the floor. Someone had written *FREE HALLOWEEN STUFF* in marker on the side of the box, and Lisa Marie could see vampire capes, devil tridents and other spooky accessories piled up inside.

"*Hello!*" cried the man. He was dressed in black and hopped from foot to foot as if he desperately needed to find the bathroom. "You're my first customers. How exciting is that?!"

"Amazing," Vernon said, but he didn't sound like he meant it. "We want a free bear."

Lisa Marie rolled her eyes. "Sorry about him," she said. She held out a hand for the shopkeeper to shake. "What happened to the Changs?"

"The what?" the shopkeeper asked.

"The previous owners," Lisa Marie answered. "Mr. and Mrs. Chang."

"Oh, them! Yes. They, uh, they retired," said the man.

"They didn't mention anything," Lisa Marie said.

The shopkeeper shrugged. "I think it was quite sudden."

"Oh, I see. Well, I'm Lisa Marie. Maybe they told you about me?"

"Warned you about her, more like," Vernon muttered.

"Uh, hi. I'm Josh," the man replied, shaking Lisa Marie's hand. "And no. No, I can't say they did."

Lisa Marie felt a twinge of disappointment at this. "Oh. Okay, then," she said. "Well, I'm a

8

regular here. And I used to re-solder the wiring on the tumble turner whenever it came loose."

Josh blinked. "Do what to the what?"

"The tumble turner," Lisa Marie said, pointing to the machine in the corner. "The stuffing machine. I used to fix it."

"Right! Yes. The tumble thing. Good. Well, then I'm very pleased to meet you, Lisa Marie," Josh said. He bowed deeply and smiled at her. "And since you're practically staff, it seems fitting that you should be the first to create your free Halloween bear."

Vernon stepped between them. "Hang on— it's not for her, it's for our dad. I mean stepdad. I mean *her* dad, my stepdad. That's why we're here."

"It's his birthday tomorrow," Lisa Marie explained. "And Vernon wants to get him a free bear so he can keep the money Mom gave him to buy a present."

"How generous," Josh said as he winked at Lisa Marie. "Still, it's the thought that counts, I suppose."

He clapped his hands together, then did a sort of sideways shuffle over to the rack of teddy-bear skins.

Lisa Marie grinned. Although she was going to miss the Changs, she was already starting to like Josh. He seemed like fun, and his glasses were quite similar to her own. Nerd goggles, Vernon called them, although she noticed he wasn't saying it now.

"Have no fear—there are free bears for *every-one!*" Josh cried. "You can make one for your dad, and your sister can make one for herself. Problem solved."

"Stepsister," Vernon corrected him. He thrust a hand into the cardboard box and yanked out a werewolf costume. "We'll take this one," he said, without even looking.

"That's not how it works," Lisa Marie said. "You pick your bear skin first, get it stuffed, put a heart in and *then* choose the outfit. Right?"

She looked up at Josh. He blinked in surprise. "Uh . . . yes. Yes! That's it. Just as she said."

Vernon threw the costume back into the box and sighed grumpily. "Fine!" He joined Lisa Marie next to the rack of bear skins. Their lifeless eyes seemed to gaze back at the children, and Vernon felt the fine hairs on the back of his neck stand up.

"This is so stupid," he muttered, but he was careful to avoid their glassy gazes.

Lisa Marie was considering her options carefully, checking every one of the skins for loose threads or other imperfections. As she did, something half hidden by the tarp caught her eye. It was shining and sparkling, and Lisa Marie recognized the outfit at once.

"Wait! Can we make a bear wearing *that* costume?" she asked, pulling the tarp aside to reveal a white jumpsuit covered in hundreds of shiny sequins.

Josh smiled, but pulled the tarpaulin back into place. "Sorry, those aren't for sale today. Halloween bears only. Did I mention they're free?"

"You did," Lisa Marie said. She tugged the plastic sheeting aside again. "But that's an Elvis costume, and my dad loves Elvis."

That was an understatement. Elvis Presley was her dad's all-time favorite singer. Dad's half of the bedroom he shared with Vernon's mom was covered in pictures, clocks and even mirrors, all bearing the face of the man Dad called the King of Rock and Roll.

"We'll pay for it," Lisa Marie said.

Vernon's ears pricked up. "Wait, what? No we won't. Why would we pay for a bear when we can get a free one?"

"Because we love Dad," Lisa Marie huffed. "And Dad loves Elvis."

She kept her gaze fixed firmly on the shop-keeper. He wrung his hands, jiggling anxiously, as if his bladder were about to blow up.

"Well, that wasn't really the plan . . . but fine," said Josh. He took the outfit down from the rack and checked the label. "I'll sell you a . . . Bearvis."

Lisa Marie raised an eyebrow. "Bearvis?"

"Probably can't use *Elvis* for legal reasons," Josh said, although he didn't seem all that sure.

"Why Bearvis, though?" Lisa Marie wondered. "That doesn't sound anything like Elvis. It sounds like Mavis, if anything."

Josh shrugged. "Well, can you think of a better bear-related pun on the name Elvis Presley?"

Lisa Marie thought for two seconds. "Elvis Grizzly," she announced.

Josh blinked. "Uh, yeah. Yeah, that is better," he admitted. He handed her the outfit. "That'll be forty dollars."

"How much?!" Vernon spluttered.

Lisa Marie reached into her purse and took out her own neatly folded twenty-dollar bill. She elbowed her brother in the ribs and nodded in Josh's direction.

Vernon groaned. "Ugh. I really hate you sometimes."

Lisa Marie smiled sweetly. "I know," she said.

Josh took the money, then held up his index finger. "You can make your Bearvis, but I have one stipulation."

"One what?" Vernon asked.

"Stipulation. It means like 'one condition,'" Lisa Marie explained.

"Well, why didn't he just say that, then?" Vernon grunted.

"Okay," Lisa Marie said, ignoring her brother. "Name it."

"You both make Halloween bears for yourselves, too," Josh said. His lips drew back into a wide smile, and the light seemed to dance across his glasses. "And you make them both *extra* scary!"

Lisa Marie studied the rack of skins again. What to choose? What to choose?

The empty teddy-bear skins somehow managed to look cute, despite being . . . well, empty teddy-bear skins. It was tricky picking one to use for a scary Halloween bear.

The orange one was nice, but a bit too bright. It reminded Lisa Marie of the woman down the street who spent all her spare time at the spray-tan salon.

The white one looked okay, but it would get dirty very easily. Lisa Marie thought practically about things like that. For the same reason, she also ruled out the light brown, the cream and the one the label called purple but was clearly rose quartz.

That left the black, the dark brown, the green or the red. The red was even brighter than the orange—so bright that it hurt her eyes just to look at it. The black was so dark you couldn't make out where the teddy's eyes were, or even if it had eyes at all. She ruled both of those out and took a look at the two remaining colors.

The dark brown had no blatant faults. It wasn't painfully bright. It wouldn't show dirt easily. The bear's eyes were clearly visible from several yards away. There was nothing *obviously* wrong with it.

Except it was boring. She already had a dozen or more brown teddy bears. She didn't need another one.

Her mind at last made up, Lisa Marie reached for the green bear and pulled it down from the rack.

"Good choice," said Josh, hopping up behind her. He jabbed a thumb in the direction of the stuffing machine. "Did you say you know how to work this?"

"Yes," Lisa Marie told him. "Why, don't you?"

"What? Me? Yeah, of course!" Josh said quickly. "I just thought you might want to do it."

Lisa Marie grinned. "Okay, if you insist!"

She ran over to the stuffing machine. Huge wads of white fluffy cotton tumbled around inside, spinning and twirling like the world's biggest cotton candy machine. Josh watched her closely as she hooked her bear skin over a metal tube and pulled the lever that would fill her teddy with stuffing.

"Have you picked one yet?" Josh called across to Vernon.

"I told you, I'm not making a stupid teddy bear." Vernon scowled. "They're for little kids."

"Ah-ah-ah!" Josh said, wagging a finger. "Remember the deal—no Halloween bear, no Bearvis."

"I didn't even want him in the first place," Vernon muttered. He sighed and snatched a red bear skin from the rack. "Fine. I'll take this one."

He headed over to join Lisa Marie by the stuffing machine, where she had just finished plumping up her bear skin with cotton. She gave it a hug to test it, then turned her attention to a small cardboard box at the side of the machine. It had no lid, and inside were hundreds upon hundreds of satin hearts. They were about as long as her thumb, and no thicker than a coin.

She picked one up, just like she'd done every other time she'd made a teddy in the shop, then thought for a moment. Giving a nod, she gave the heart a gentle kiss. "Henrietta," she whispered, which made her brother erupt into loud laughter.

"Henrietta?" he snorted. "What sort of name is that?"

"It's a good name," Lisa Marie insisted. "It's a better name than whatever you come up with."

"I'm not picking a name. And I'm not kissing any stupid heart, either," Vernon grunted.

"Well, hurry up and get its stuffing in," Josh said, placing his hands on Vernon's shoulders and steering him toward the part of the machine that dispensed the cotton. "Then we can get to the good part: dressing up!"

It had taken Lisa Marie some time to decide on the color of her bear, but she didn't have the same problem choosing a costume.

There were dozens of Halloween-themed costumes in the cardboard box, but after only a few moments rummaging through them, Lisa Marie settled on the one she wanted.

The outfit's tiny hat was black and pointed, with a wide brim. A plastic spider dangled from the very tip on a thin length of thread. A matching black dress hung below the hat—ragged and torn at the very bottom. Completing the outfit were a small plastic broomstick and an even smaller wooden wand.

"A witch?" said Vernon. "How *original*."

"Oh, and I suppose you're making something spectacular, are you?" Lisa Marie replied. "Something the world has never seen before."

"Maybe I am!"

Vernon tipped over the box, spilling the contents onto the floor. There were clothes for werewolves, demons and vampires; outfits for ghosts, ghouls, goblins and gremlins, and all manner of mean-looking accessories.

The box also contained bandages for mummies, eye patches for pirates and jetpacks for aliens. There was slime for the slime beasts, boogers for the bogeymen and plastic axes for the axe-wielding maniacs. "You said this stuff's free, right?" Vernon asked.

"That's right," said Josh.

Vernon smiled and snatched up seven or eight items at random, then carried them over to the dress-up table. "Right," he told his sister. "Just wait and see what I come up with!"

3

That night, when the sun had gone down and a full moon hung in the sky, something dark and sinister tiptoed down the stairs of Lisa Marie and Vernon's house. It crept across the hall, its long black cape swishing soundlessly behind it.

The figure had almost reached the front door when a voice shouted from the living room.

"Vernon, is that you?"

Vernon groaned. So close. He'd been *so* close.

"Yeah, it's me," he said. With a final longing glance at the front door, he poked his head into the living room.

Mom was at the coffee table, tipping tasty-looking colored candy into a big bowl. Vernon's stepdad, Steve, was kneeling on the floor in front of Lisa Marie, helping her get dressed up as . . . Actually, what was she getting dressed up as? With her gray hair and brown suit, she looked more like an old man than some horrifying Halloween monster.

"Forget you were taking Lisa Marie out, did you?" Mom said, smiling in a way that suggested she already knew the answer to her question.

"Aw, yeah, I did forget," Vernon lied, his words coming out slurred because of his plastic vampire teeth. He spat them into his hand. "I've arranged to meet up with the guys. Sorry."

"Well, Lisa Marie's friends are away, so she's got no one to go with."

"I'll be fine on my own," Lisa Marie said.

"No way," said Dad, tucking one of her braids up under her wig. "You're not going trick-or-treating on your own."

"But I said I'd meet the guys!" Vernon protested.

"Oh, far be it from us to stop you from meeting your friends," said Mom.

Vernon reeled in surprise. "Really? Awesome! Thanks, Mom."

She smirked. "But you're taking your sister with you."

"I am so sick of babysitting you all the time, you know that?"

Lisa Marie trotted along the sidewalk, trying to keep up with Vernon's much longer strides. "I know."

"I've got things to do," Vernon grumbled. "I shouldn't be stuck looking after . . . looking after . . ." He stopped and studied his stepsister's costume. "What exactly are you supposed to be, anyway?"

"Thomas Edison." Lisa Marie beamed, smoothing down her gray wig. "He invented the lightbulb."

Vernon shook his head and continued walking. "It's Halloween." He sighed. "You're supposed to be something scary."

"You don't *have* to be something scary," Lisa Marie replied.

"Yes you do! That's the whole point! Why do you think I'm dressed as Dracula?"

"Um . . . because you always go as Dracula?" Lisa Marie guessed.

"Exactly!" Vernon cried. "Because you're supposed to go as something scary! I'm a vampire. I'm a terrifying, unkillable monster!"

"You can kill a vampire," Lisa Marie countered.

"What? No you can't!"

"A stake through the heart kills a vampire. One quick jab in the chest with a sharp piece of wood does the trick. According to Bram Stoker, anyway."

"Who?"

"Bram Stoker. He wrote *Dracula*," Lisa Marie explained. "Some people think fire kills them too, although there's some debate about it. They think it kills vampires, I mean, not authors." She considered this. "But probably authors as well."

Vernon shook his head in despair and looked Lisa Marie up and down. He was dressed as the most evil vampire who had ever lived; she was an old man in a brown suit. She looked ridiculous.

"Anyway, if Edison hadn't invented the lightbulb, then it'd be dark all the time," Lisa Marie said with a shudder. "Now, *that* would be scary!"

Vernon sighed. "Is he dead? The guy you're supposed to be?"

"Thomas Edison," Lisa Marie answered. "Yes, he is."

"Good. You can be his ghost, then. If anyone asks, you're Thomas Whatsisname's ghost, okay?"

Lisa Marie shrugged. "Okay."

"Right, then." Vernon stuck in his plastic fangs and turned up the path of the first house on his carefully planned route. "Let's go get some candy!"

Two hours later, their bags filled to bursting with nuts, apples and all kinds of candy, Vernon and Lisa Marie headed home.

"If I drop you off now, I can probably still meet up with the guys," Vernon muttered. "Maybe— just maybe—you won't have completely ruined my night."

Lisa Marie nodded but didn't reply. They walked on in silence for a few moments. All around them, the sounds of laughter and Halloween high jinks echoed from distant streets.

"Thanks for this," Lisa Marie said.

"For what?"

"For taking me out. I know you didn't want to."

"Oh." Vernon rolled his eyes. "Whatever."

"And thanks for letting us get Bearvis too. Mom says Dad will love him. She's wrapped the box and put it in the living room cabinet so we can surprise him with it tomorrow."

Vernon nodded. "Right."

"I told her you insisted we buy it," Lisa Marie continued. "And that you didn't get any change. She was so impressed I think she's going to give you extra pocket money."

"Why did you tell her that?" Vernon asked.

"Because you're my brother." Lisa Marie shrugged. "And I know you wanted that money."

"I'm not your . . . ," Vernon began, but stopped when he saw the sad look dart across her face. He sighed.

"You know something?" he said. "Sometimes, I suppose you're actually . . ."

Lisa Marie waited for him to finish the sentence. "I'm what?" she asked at last.

"Uh, nothing. Just be quiet," Vernon said, his voice dropping to a whisper.

"What? Why?"

"All right, Vern?" called a red-faced demon. He was stalking along the street toward them, a pack of zombies and skeletons close behind.

"Oh, of course." Lisa Marie sighed. "Better not say anything nice to me in front of your *friends*. Whatever would they think?"

"All right, Drake?" Vernon said, and grinned too enthusiastically for it to be natural.

"Not bad, Vern, not bad," Drake replied. He snatched Lisa Marie's bag from her and peered inside. "Nice haul," he said, nodding his approval.

"Hey! Give that back!" Lisa Marie cried.

"No chance," hissed Drake. "Go home, little girl. This is mine now." Behind him, his gang giggled like hungry hyenas.

"But I spent all night collecting that!"

"That," said Drake, unwrapping a piece of candy and popping it in his mouth, "is your problem, not mine."

Lisa Marie looked up at her brother. "Vernon, tell him!" she pleaded. "He's taking my treats!"

Vernon opened his mouth to say something, but when he saw the expression on Drake's face, he felt his mouth go dry. When he spoke, he could barely hide the tremor in his voice. "You heard him, Lisa Marie," he said. "Go home."

Lisa Marie stared at Vernon for a few moments, too shocked to move. Around her, the gang's laughter seemed impossibly loud.

"Come on, let's go egg old Grindley's house," Drake announced. He turned and began to march off, Lisa Marie already forgotten.

Vernon moved to follow, then stopped. He looked down at his bag of candy, then back at his sister. Without a word, he thrust the bag at her, smiling weakly as she took it, then scampered off after Drake and the others.

A few hours later, when everyone was tucked in for the night, Lisa Marie lay curled in her bed, watching the hands of her clock creep around and listening to the faint hum of her night-light.

There was only a minute until midnight—one minute left of Halloween—and she still couldn't get to sleep. She hated not being able to sleep. It usually meant she was cranky all the next day, and she didn't want to be cranky on Dad's birthday.

As the final few moments of Halloween drained away, Lisa Marie yawned, shut her eyes tight and cuddled Henrietta, her new bear. Even dressed as a witch, the teddy looked adorable. Not like Vernon's bear. For a stuffed toy, it had been terrifying, and Vernon had actually seemed quite proud of it right up until the point he'd tossed it into his bedroom and made Lisa Marie promise never to tell anyone he'd made it.

Henrietta felt oddly warm, like a hot-water bottle, as Lisa Marie snuggled her close.

And then, with just one second to go until midnight, Lisa Marie finally drifted off to sleep, blissfully unaware of the horrors she was about to encounter.

THUMP.

Lisa Marie flicked open her eyes but otherwise didn't move a muscle. She was facing the clock on her bedside table, and saw that its hands pointed to quarter past twelve. She'd been asleep for only fifteen minutes, so why had she woken up?

THUMP.

Her breath caught at the back of her throat. Something was in the room with her, moving around. Usually, Lisa Marie was a sensible girl, but right there and then, she could think only one thing: monsters!

She shut her eyes so tightly that she could see colors dancing behind her lids, and hugged Henrietta harder than ever.

Or at least, she tried to, but the teddy was no longer in her arms. The witch bear must've fallen out of bed while Lisa Marie was asleep.

THUMP.

This time, she felt the bed shake. She gave a little gasp of shock as her duvet began to move. Someone was pulling it down toward the bottom of the bed!

Quickly, Lisa Marie sat up. She opened her mouth to scream, but her throat was blocked by terror, and no sound came out. She gaped down at the end of the bed, unsure what she'd see in the glow of her night-light, but fearing that it would be something terrible.

What she saw was . . . nothing at all. Everything looked just as it had before she'd fallen asleep: The neat stack of clothes. The chessboard. The shelves of alphabetically arranged books.

Her room was just her room, with not a monster in sight.

Lisa Marie shook herself—she was being silly. Monsters weren't real; everyone knew that. And yet something had pulled down her duvet.

There was no other choice—she had to investigate. If she was going to be able to get back to sleep, she had to get up and check the end of her bed.

"There's nothing there," she whispered to herself as she took her glasses from the bedside table and slipped them on. She swung her bare feet down to the floor, her heart thudding in her chest like a bass drum.

B-BOOM. B-BOOM. B-BOOM.

Clenching her hands into tight, sweaty fists, Lisa Marie tiptoed to the bottom of her bed and cautiously peered underneath. A familiar figure lay limply on the floor, smiling up at her.

"Henrietta," Lisa Marie whispered, the word coming out like a giggle of relief. She bent down and scooped up the bear. "How did you get so far out of bed?"

Henrietta's green face suddenly twisted into an angry snarl. "How d'you think?" she growled. The witch bear brought its tiny broomstick up and whacked Lisa Marie on the head with the wooden end. "I flew, stupid!"

Lisa Marie released her grip on the bear. Henrietta dropped to the floor and quickly shot under the bed, out of sight.

Lisa Marie stood there, frozen in shock. Common sense told her she had to be dreaming, but the bump she could feel forming on her forehead told her she was very much awake. There was only one way to know for sure which was correct.

Slowly, she bent down and peered into the darkness beneath the wooden bed frame. She could see another stack of books, a marble and the roller skates she'd been looking for all week, but there was no sign of Henrietta. Maybe this *was* a dream after all.

With a *whoosh,* a green and black shape exploded from beneath the bed, slicing through the air on a flying broomstick. Henrietta cackled loudly as she swooped around the room, banking and curving to avoid hitting the ceiling and walls.

"Such a nice girl. Such a *tidy* girl," the bear snarled. "That won't do at all!"

The witch bear reached into her cloak and produced her miniature magic wand. With a flick of her wrist, she sent a bolt of blue energy crackling across the room. As it hit Lisa Marie's bookcase, the books began to launch themselves off the shelves one after the other. They flapped frantically for a few moments, before gravity brought them thumping down onto the floor.

"My books!" Lisa Marie cried. "Not my books!"

Henrietta's furry face sneered. *"Oh, not my precious books!"* she cackled wickedly. "If you think that's bad, just wait and see what I'm going to do to all your stupid science sets!"

"Don't you dare!" Lisa Marie yelped, then spun around as the door to her bedroom was thrown open. Mom and Dad stood in the doorway, looking a bit sleepy and a lot annoyed.

"Lisa Marie," snapped Dad. "What on earth is all the noise ab—?"

A bolt of magical energy shot from Henrietta's wand and hit Dad on the chest of his checked pajamas. His whole body seemed to light up for a fraction of a second; then he was lost in a cloud of smoke.

When the cloud cleared, only his slippers remained. As a terror-stricken Mom and Lisa Marie watched, a tiny green frog hopped from one of the slippers, looked down at its new body and gave quite a sad-sounding "Ribbit."

"And for my next trick . . . ," shrieked Henrietta. She spun upside down on her broomstick to avoid the lampshade and launched another magical bolt at Mom.

One flash of light and a puff of smoke later, Mom, too, had gone. In her place sat a fat, juicy slug. The slug slowly turned its slimy head to look up at the frog. The frog gazed down at the slug. Although Lisa Marie had very little experience reading the facial expressions of frogs, she thought this one was starting to look quite hungry.

"Change them back!" ordered Lisa Marie. "Change them back right now!"

"Oh, I don't think so, my pretty!" roared Henrietta. "Now that they're like this, they won't be able to stop me from robbing the place."

She banked sharply and swooped toward Lisa Marie. The witch bear's eyes glowed a spooky shade of green as she took aim with her wand. "And in a moment, neither will you!"

Lisa Marie dropped to her knees, barely avoiding a bright blue blast of magic. Behind her, her dressing table found itself suddenly transformed into a very small, very confused guinea pig. It paused for a moment to glance at its surroundings, then quietly began eating the carpet.

As Henrietta swung around for another attack, Lisa Marie made her move. She rolled forward, scooping up the frog with one hand and the slug with the other. They both felt disgusting against her skin, but there was no time to worry about that.

Stumbling, she ran from her room into Vernon's, which was directly across the landing. Hooking her leg around Vernon's door, she slammed it shut behind her.

A second later, she heard a thud and a muffled "Ooyah!" as Henrietta crashed hard against the solid wood.

Vernon was asleep, snoring softly. Lisa Marie shook her head. That boy could sleep through anything.

"Wake up," she hissed, giving him a gentle kick. "Vernon, wake up!"

"Wha—?" Vernon muttered. He half opened one eye. "Wha' you doin'?" he slurred. "G'back t'sleep."

"Look!" Lisa Marie cried. She held out the frog so it was right next to his face. It looked up at him, lazily licking its own eyeballs.

Vernon screamed and leaped out of bed. "Get it away! Get it away!" he yelped. "Why've you brought a frog into my room, you weirdo? Mom! Steve!"

"This *is* Steve! Dad, I mean," Lisa Marie told him. She held out the slug. "And this is Mom."

Vernon looked at the frog. He looked at the slug. He looked at his stepsister. "You're nuts," he said at last. "You're out of your mind." Shaking his head, he made for the bedroom door. "I'm telling Mom."

"*DON'T OPEN THE DOOR!*"

Something in Lisa Marie's voice made Vernon stop. He stood there, his hand resting on the door handle. "Why not?"

"Because my Halloween teddy bear is out there," squeaked Lisa Marie. "And it's alive!" She stepped closer to her stepbrother. He was looking at her, his eyes wide and staring. "I know you probably don't believe me, but please trust me, you've . . . you've . . ."

She studied Vernon's face and realized that he wasn't looking at her at all. He was looking past her, at something across the room.

Lisa Marie turned, following Vernon's gaze. Her stepbrother's Halloween costume lay in a crumpled heap on the floor. Nothing unusual there. Crumpled heap was Vernon's normal method of storing his clothes. What *was* unusual about this particular crumpled heap was that it was moving.

"What's under there?" Lisa Marie whispered.

Vernon shook his head, unable to believe what he was seeing. "The teddy bear," he whimpered. "That stupid teddy I made at the shop."

"It must be alive too!" Lisa Marie gasped.

"Shut up. It can't be," Vernon muttered. "It . . . it . . ." His voice trailed off as he remembered exactly what he'd made at the Create-a-Ted shop.

He would be the first to admit he'd gotten a little carried away when building his free Halloween bear. The armful of items he'd selected had contained a whole range of monster parts. He'd started off making a vampire, then added a dash of zombie, a smidgen of demon and several other pieces from a few of the scarier costumes. He'd mixed and matched them all to create the most terrifying teddy bear the world had ever seen.

The teddy bear that was now under his Halloween costume.

Moving.

"N-no," he stammered. "It can't be alive. It can't!"

Rrrrrip! The children leaped back as the vampire cape was torn in two. A set of curved werewolf claws emerged from within the dark folds of the cloak, followed a moment later by a hideous, fur-covered head.

"Whoa!" cried the teddy bear as it pulled itself free. It stumbled across to Vernon's full-length mirror and studied its reflection, barely paying the children the slightest bit of attention.

The bear bent this way and that, checking itself out. Vernon really had gone wild with the accessories. Two demon horns poked from the bear's furry forehead. Its cheeks were sunken and rotting, like the undead flesh of a zombie. Glowing red eyes and yellowing vampire fangs completed a face that Lisa Marie knew would appear in every one of her future nightmares.

Each of the bear's paws ended in four razor-sharp werewolf claws, while a little see-through ghostly tail curled out from roughly where its spine would end, if teddy bears had spines.

Its clothing was a bizarre mishmash of vampire, pirate, warlock and alien. If the costume was a fashion statement, that statement would simply be "Run away!"

Lisa Marie realized she was still holding her mom and dad. She tucked them out of sight behind her back, just in case the teddy decided to eat them.

"I like it," said the bear. "I look like one scary dude!" It fixed the children with a demonic glare. "Which one of you meatbags put me together?"

"She did!" Vernon pointed.

"What?!" spluttered Lisa Marie. "I did not!"

The bear threw back its head and laughed. The sound seemed to echo around the room. "Nice try, kid. Devious. I like it."

"Wh-who are you?" Lisa Marie stammered.

"Good question," said the bear. It moved closer to the children and stared up at Vernon. "You didn't give me a name. A bear needs a name."

Vernon gulped as he desperately tried to think of a name that might please the monstrous teddy. "Um . . . Duncan?" he said at last.

The bear blinked. "Duncan? Do I look like a Duncan?"

"Keith?" Vernon suggested, his voice coming out as a squeak.

"Try harder," the bear growled.

Vernon swallowed. "Um . . . um . . . Grizz?"

"Grizz," said the teddy, letting the R roll around at the back of its throat. "I like it. Grizz it is."

A burst of flame seemed to flicker briefly behind the bear's eyes. "Now, down to business," he said. There was a **RRRIP** as Grizz tore Vernon's game console out from under his TV, snapping the cable. He looked it over, then shrugged. "This'll do."

"Um . . . ," Vernon mumbled. He wanted to protest, but something about the bear—or more accurately, *everything* about the bear—told him he probably shouldn't.

Grizz tucked the console under one stubby arm, then winked at Lisa Marie and Vernon. "See you around, meatbags," he spat.

And then, with a flash of demon magic, he was gone.

Lisa Marie had never seen anyone faint before. Not in real life, anyway.

It was quite interesting watching her big brother's face as he fell backward on to his bed. His skin turned a shade of gray, his eyeballs sort of rolled up in his head and his tongue flopped out. Lisa Marie would've quite liked to have taken a picture, but she didn't have a camera and her hands were full of slimy creatures, so she couldn't.

She leaned over and poked him with her foot.

"Vernon? Vernon, wake up," she said, but Vernon just snored in reply.

There was no denying it—her brother had definitely fainted.

"My hero," Lisa Marie muttered.

A less practical girl, confronted with the same circumstances, would have panicked. Lisa Marie did panic, but only a little, and not for very long. Panicking, she knew, got you nowhere.

First things first: she had to put Mom and Dad somewhere safe. After that she could concentrate on the other problems—namely, her unconscious stepbrother and the evil witch bear probably still lurking right outside the door.

Then there was the whole "teddy bears coming to life" thing. That would be a biggie.

Somewhere along the line she'd have to find a way to change her parents back to normal, of course—it was parents' night at school soon, and they could hardly go looking like they did at the moment. For now, though, she'd settle for finding somewhere safe to put them.

She toppled Vernon's box of old action figures with a kick, spilling the contents across the floor. Righting the plastic box with her foot, Lisa Marie gently lowered her mom and dad inside. Dad gave a loud "ribbit." If Mom said anything, she didn't say it loudly enough for anyone to hear.

"Okay, this won't be for long," Lisa Marie explained, looking around for the box's clip-on lid. It'd had a crack almost from one side to the other since last Christmas Eve, when she and Vernon had used it to go sledding. The split was wide enough to let air in, so her parents wouldn't suffocate.

Before she closed the lid, Lisa Marie gazed down at the frog and the slug. They stared back at her. The frog had a sad, scared look on its face. The slug . . . well, the slug was just a slug. It wasn't giving much away, emotion-wise.

"I promise we'll change you back," she whispered, adjusting her glasses, which had slipped down a little on her nose. "You won't be this way for long, okay?" She gave them a warm smile and clicked the lid of the box into place.

A second later, she opened it again. "Oh, and by the way," she said, staring sternly at the frog, "Mom is *not* food!"

With that taken care of, Lisa Marie moved on to priority number two—Henrietta. If she was left to her own devices, there was no telling what sort of mischief the witch bear would get up to. Lisa Marie had made her, so it was Lisa Marie's job to make sure she didn't hurt anyone else. Besides, if there was a way to turn her parents back, Henrietta would probably know it.

Grabbing Vernon's tennis racket from the floor, Lisa Marie edged open the bedroom door and peeked out. Her eyes swiveled as she scanned the hallway. Henrietta was nowhere to be seen.

Cautiously, she pulled the door open farther and stepped out onto the landing, holding the tennis racket poised and ready to start swinging.

Nothing. No evil cackle. No bolt of magic. No Henrietta.

At the top of the stairs, Lisa Marie paused. She could hear movement down there. Thudding. Muttering. The sound of someone trying to move something heavy.

Glancing back to check on Vernon, Lisa Marie rested a hand on the banister and began to creep down the stairs.

The closer she got to the bottom, the louder the sounds became. The muttering voice was

Henrietta's, she was sure of it, but what was the witch bear doing?

Slowly, with the racket held before her like a shield, Lisa Marie leaned around the doorframe. Henrietta was half carrying, half dragging the TV across the floor, trailing the power cable behind her.

"P-put that back," Lisa Marie instructed.

The television toppled sideways as Henrietta clambered out from beneath it. Screeching, she launched herself at Lisa Marie, spitting and snarling. Lisa Marie swished wildly with the racket, but the witch bear was too fast. Henrietta shrieked with delight as she caught hold of Lisa Marie's hair and swung around onto the girl's back.

Yelping in shock, Lisa Marie twisted and turned, trying to force the fuzzy witch to release her grip, but Henrietta hung on tightly, howling with laughter as Lisa Marie flailed around and around and around.

"Get off!" Lisa Marie cried.

To her surprise, the witch bear did just that. Henrietta stuck a paw in her mouth and let out a shrill whistle as she tumbled through the air, summoning her broomstick. It zipped out from its hiding place behind the couch and caught her mid-fall.

"Impressive, huh?" the bear cackled.

The broomstick banked left before curving around and down and clipping Lisa Marie on the back of the knees. Lisa Marie squealed as she was thrown off-balance and landed hard on the floor.

Frantically, Lisa Marie spun onto her back. Henrietta leaped from her broomstick and dropped onto the fallen girl's stomach, knocking the breath from her. The witch's wand bristled with energy in her paw.

"Now, my little Goody Two-shoes," Henrietta spat. "Let's see if we can think of something *really disgusting* to change you into!"

"Help!" Lisa Marie cried, unsure of what else to do at this point. "Vernon! Anyone! Someone, help me!"

"There's no one coming to help you, little girl," hissed Henrietta. The witch leaned in close and grinned, revealing a mouthful of brown and black teeth. "You hear that, my pretty? No one is coming. No one is coming to save—"

Thump. A sound from the cupboard cut Henrietta's sentence short. The witch bear frowned.

Thump. Both she and Lisa Marie turned their eyes toward the cupboard door.

Thump.

Thump.

THUMP!

On the fifth thump, the door swung open and a gift-wrapped box toppled out. It landed on the floor and lay there, motionless. Henrietta eyed it suspiciously. Only when she was sure it had stopped moving did she turn her attention back to the girl.

"Now," she said, sneering. "Where were we?"

Suddenly, the box began to bounce violently up and down. It shook and shuddered this way and that, as if controlled by some crazed invisible force.

"Are you doing that?" Henrietta scowled.

Lisa Marie shook her head.

"Well, *someone's* doing it!" hissed the witch. "And it isn't me!"

With a final bounce, something furry and sparkling erupted from the parcel. It somersaulted in the air before landing near Lisa Marie's head.

With the moonlight glinting off the sequins of his suit, the newly arrived teddy bear ran a paw through his thick jet-black pompadour and curled his upper lip into the beginnings of a playful sneer.

The bear gave Lisa Marie a short but friendly nod. "Well, hey there, little darlin'," he drawled in a deep Southern accent. "Looks to me like you could use a little help."

Number three on Lisa Marie's top five list of favorite words was *agog*. It meant "awestruck," or "eager and excited." She loved the word, but didn't believe she'd ever actually *been* agog.

Until now.

"Elvis!" she gasped, staring wide-eyed at the teddy.

"Bearvis!" hissed Henrietta, jumping off Lisa Marie and onto the carpet.

The new arrival glanced at them both. "How about y'all just call me the King?"

Henrietta narrowed her eyes and growled. "How about we call you Dead Ted instead?"

Giggling wickedly, she gave her wand a flick. A shimmering ball of magical energy zipped from

59

the end. Quick as a flash, the King held up a paw. The magic bolt hit the shiny gold rings he wore on his stubby fingers, bounced back and blasted Henrietta across the room.

Lisa Marie found herself holding the witch's tiny wand. It tingled with magical energy.

She sat up and watched as the witch began to change. The green fur that covered the evil teddy from head to toe was falling out in chunks as she took on a sickly, slimy appearance.

"I'm molting! I'm *molting*!" Henrietta wailed, the final tufts of her fur drifting down onto the living room carpet. A scant second later, the bear was gone. In her place a plump, see-through jellyfish wobbled gently back and forth.

In the silence that followed, the King gave a low whistle. "Well now," he said. "That sure ain't somethin' you see every day."

Lisa Marie scrambled to her feet and backed away from the shiny-suited bear. "You're alive!" she cried. Then a thought struck her. "Wait. You're on my side, right? You're not going to change me into something slimy, are you?"

The King's furry face took on a puzzled expression. "Darlin'," he replied, "I wouldn't even know where to start. I ain't one for magic, but I guess I could sing to you."

"*Sing* to me?"

"Well, sure thing, honey, since you asked so nicely. How's about 'A Little Less Hibernation'? You heard that one?"

"What's going on?" asked Vernon, appearing in the doorway. He yawned and stretched. "I just had a really weird dream about—"

He stopped when he spotted Bearvis. The little bear tapped a paw to his brow in salute. "Hey there, son. Y'all look like you've seen a ghost."

The King and Lisa Marie both watched in silence as Vernon's eyes rolled backward again. He landed with a thud in the hall.

"Uh, is he okay?" the King asked.

Lisa Marie sighed. "Yes. He does that."

She lowered herself onto the arm of the couch and looked Bearvis up and down. He wasn't very tall, so it didn't take long. "You're alive," she said.

"Sure looks that way, honey," Bearvis agreed.

"But *how*?"

The King shrugged his fluffy shoulders. "Can't say I know the answer to that. I wasn't alive, and now I am. That's about all I can tell you." He frowned. "Although I think there was some kinda machine involved? I don't rightly remember."

"TEDDIES!" roared Vernon, jumping awake.

The sudden shout took Lisa Marie by surprise. She turned around, startled. The abrupt movement somehow made the wand go off in her hand. A bolt of energy streaked across the room and hit Vernon right on the end of his chin.

There was a flash and a puff of smoke. Lisa Marie gasped as Vernon flopped backward onto the floor again.

"Whoops!" she whispered.

"Uh, did you mean to blast that guy with magic?" the King asked.

"He's my brother. And no," said Lisa Marie.

"Right. Right," replied the King. "Because you did. In case you hadn't noticed."

"I noticed," said Lisa Marie. She crept closer to her brother. "Uh, Vernon? Vernon, are you okay?"

Vernon groaned and sat up. "I'm fine," he said. "What hit me?"

Lisa Marie stared. She knew it was rude, but she couldn't help herself. Behind her, she heard the King let out a low whistle.

"The bear!" said Vernon, pointing to Bearvis. "The bear's alive!"

"Yes," Lisa Marie said, her eyes widening. "But he's on our side."

"On our side? So . . . what? This *isn't* a dream?"

"No," Lisa Marie said.

"Why are you staring at me?" Vernon asked, finally spotting the look of wonder on his sister's face. "What's wrong?"

"Your head," said Lisa Marie.

"What about it?"

"It's . . . big."

Vernon stood up. This was quite difficult because he was finding it tricky to balance properly. He stumbled past Lisa Marie and looked at himself in the mirror above the fireplace.

He screamed.

"My head!"

"I know," Lisa Marie said.

"It's *huge*!"

"You can say that again," said the King. "That's the biggest head I ever saw. And it ain't a close-run thing."

Vernon's head had inflated like a very large, very round balloon. It was easily three times as big as normal, and wobbled unsteadily on his normal-sized neck.

Lisa Marie bit her bottom lip. Vernon's huge face had gone that ash-gray color once more, and

he looked like he might be about to faint again. "Don't panic. Deep breaths. It's fine," she said. "It looks . . . good."

"*Good?!*" Vernon cried. "It's the size of the moon!"

"Actually, the moon has a circumference of almost seven thousand miles—" Lisa Marie began, but the scowl on her brother's massive face stopped her. "I take your point."

"How did this happen?" Vernon groaned, turning back to the mirror.

Bearvis stepped forward. "Well, you see that wand there?" he said. Lisa Marie gestured for him to be quiet, but it was too late.

"*You* did this?!" Vernon spat. He wobbled toward her. "Then fix me!"

Lisa Marie looked down at the wand in her hand, then back at her humongous-headed brother. "I don't know how to."

"Figure it out!" Vernon snapped. "I can't be stuck like this."

Taking a deep breath, Lisa Marie nodded. "Okay. I'll try. How difficult can it be?"

"Well, actually," Bearvis began, but Lisa Marie ignored him. She raised the wand and flicked her wrist. A bolt of blue energy hit Vernon's mega-sized forehead.

"Ow!" he protested, stumbling back. He placed his hands on his head and laughed. "It's working! It's working!"

And it was. Vernon's head was already shrinking. It took just a few seconds to shrink back to its normal size.

Unfortunately, it didn't stop there.

"Make it stop!" cried Vernon, his voice now squeaky and high-pitched. His head was the size of a grapefruit, and still shrinking.

Lisa Marie flicked the wand again. There was a flash and a bang, and Vernon's head snapped back to the correct size.

That was the good news.

"It's back-to-front!" Vernon protested.

That was the bad news.

"Hold on. I'll get it this time," Lisa Marie said. Before Vernon could stop her, she gave the wand another flick.

When the flash of light had passed, Vernon's head was the right size and facing the correct way. He prodded it cautiously, as if scared it might explode.

"Okay. Okay. Thank you," he wheezed, once he was sure his skull was back to normal. He breathed in through his nose and pulled himself together. "Now put that thing away before you do any more damage!"

Lisa Marie decided this was probably sensible, and tucked the wand into the waistband of her pajamas.

"Good," Vernon said. "Now can someone *please* tell me what's going on?"

The King was over by the window, only his bottom half visible beneath the curtains. "Well, son," he said, stepping out and pulling a curtain aside to reveal the street beyond. Hundreds of bears swarmed along the darkened road, each dressed in different Halloween costumes. "It's funny you should ask."

There was silence for several seconds as both Lisa Marie and Vernon gazed at all the furry figures running, shuffling and flying around outside.

A moment later, the silence was broken by a soft thud as Vernon fainted, face-first, onto the carpet.

Although watching her brother faint had been interesting the first time, it was rapidly becoming annoying. Lisa Marie got a glass of cold water from the kitchen and poured it over Vernon's head.

"Urgh! Cut it out! Stop it!" he protested, rolling out of the puddle on the floor.

"I'll stop pouring water on you if you stop fainting," Lisa Marie urged. She was using her sternest voice, the one she saved for emergencies. "Pull yourself together."

"I'd listen to your sister," Bearvis suggested.

"Stepsister," Vernon corrected him automatically.

"Whatever. Sounds like she means business."

Vernon looked down at the smiling sequin-suited bear and felt his head go light again. He breathed deeply, bringing his panic under control.

"Um, okay," he mumbled. "I'm all right. This is just a bit . . . weird." Then he turned to Lisa Marie. "And we're *sure* this isn't a dream?"

Bearvis punched him on the thigh. "Ow!" Vernon yelped. "That hurt!"

"Then it looks like it ain't no dream," the King said.

Lisa Marie had crept over to the window and was now peering out from behind the curtains. The bears were still outside. Hundreds of them. Maybe *thousands,* all crisscrossing in different directions.

A pack of foot-tall zombie bears shuffled along the pavement to the left. A gang of vampire bears skulked along the road on the right, their capes billowing in the wind. Werewolf bears darted this way and that, occasionally stopping to howl at the moon or to pee against the lampposts.

Above the street, the air was filled with ghost bears, witch bears and flying alien bears all zipping around, trying not to crash into each other.

"What's going on?" Lisa Marie wondered.

"Ain't nothin' good," the King said. "I don't like the look of those guys one little bit."

"Maybe they're not all bad," Lisa Marie reasoned. "You aren't."

"Yeah, but I ain't got fangs or claws or some such. Those guys got them and more. They're bad news. I can feel it in my bones."

"You don't have bones," Lisa Marie pointed out.

"That's true, little darlin'," the King conceded. "But I got a bad feeling all the same."

One of the aliens swooped past the window on a jetpack. Lisa Marie ducked out of sight and held her breath, waiting to see if the bear was going to turn back.

"D'you think it saw us?" she whispered.

Bearvis shook his head, making his dark hair flop around. "If it saw us, I reckon it would have hit us with some crazy Zap-o-Matic Death Ray," he mumbled. "Turned us to ashes, quick as you could say 'peanut butter and banana sandwich.'"

Vernon crawled to the window and peeked out so just the top of his head was showing above the sill. "This is nuts," he said.

Lisa Marie couldn't really argue with that.

"What are they carrying?" Vernon asked.

Lisa Marie squinted. She'd been looking so closely at the bears that she hadn't noticed the items they were carrying or dragging along behind them. A few had game consoles tucked under their arms, just like Grizz had done with Vernon's. Others were pulling televisions along by their power cables or carrying stacks of phones and tablets. A few were decked out in expensive-looking necklaces. Unlike the trinkets the King wore, these were all too large for the bears, and dragged along the ground at their feet.

"They're pilfering stuff," Lisa Marie realized. *Pilfering* was another of her favorite words and one she felt she didn't use often enough.

"They're what?" Vernon asked.

"Stealing," Lisa Marie explained. She pointed down the street to where a Frankenstein's monster bear was shuffling out of a house carrying a laptop computer. "They're stealing everything!"

"Wait, I'm remembering something," said Bearvis. He placed his paws on either side of his head and concentrated. "We were all given some kinda hypnotic command or some such. I'm supposed to be robbing the place."

Lisa Marie gasped. "You wouldn't!"

"Course not, honey. I ain't no bad guy," the

King assured her. He pointed to the window. "Unlike them."

"Of course! They must assume the personalities of whatever they're wearing," Lisa Marie realized.

"They must what?" Vernon asked.

"If they look evil, they turn evil," Lisa Marie said. "That's why Bearvis is on our side, while the rest of them are looting the town."

She drew herself up to her full height. "We have to stop them."

"And how are we supposed to do that?" Vernon asked. "There are loads of them!"

Lisa Marie thought for a moment. "We could call the police," she said, but she didn't sound very sure about that.

"And say what?" asked Vernon. "That teddy bears have come to life, turned our mom and dad into slugs and are now stealing all our neighbors' stuff?"

"And your stuff," Lisa Marie pointed out.

Vernon gasped, suddenly remembering. "My console! That stupid bear took my console!"

"And they're not both slugs," Lisa Marie added. "Dad's a frog."

"Oh, well, that's *much* better!" Vernon yelped, his voice creeping higher.

"Now, don't you fret there, son. The King's gonna figure out how to put all this right," Bearvis said. He was pacing in front of the sofa and stroking his chin. "Just let me think for a second."

Lisa Marie swallowed. "Uh, King . . . ?"

"Don't you worry about nothin', little darlin'," said the bear. "I'm gonna take care of this business, quick as a flash."

"But—"

"I swear, a plan's gonna pop right into my head here any second. I can feel it a-brewin' in there, just waitin' to come out."

"Bearvis!" Lisa Marie hissed the word, almost making the teddy jump out of his fur. He turned to look at her, then instantly froze. Through the gap in the curtains they saw a gray-furred bear hovering on its shiny silver jetpack. It fixed all three of the house's occupants with a cold, calculating stare.

"I was trying to tell you," Lisa Marie gulped. "The alien. It came back!"

The King nodded. His eyes were locked on the deadly-looking weapon in the flying bear's paw. "And I'm guessing *that*," Bearvis mumbled, "has gotta be its Zap-o-Matic Death Ray."

Josh, the new owner of Create-a-Ted, yelped in surprise when a little red-furred bear wearing a mishmash of Halloween costumes and carrying an Xbox under one arm appeared in a puff of crimson smoke in the middle of the shop.

"Whoa, that was quick," he said, squinting down at Grizz over the top of his thick-rimmed glasses. He rubbed his hands together. "And ooh, you've brought me a present!"

Grizz looked down at the console, as if only just remembering it was there. He raised an arm and let it drop to the ground.

"Careful," Josh warned, scooping the console up and cradling it to his chest. "It's not worth anything broken."

Grizz shrugged. "You ask me, it ain't worth anything now." He turned and took in the shop, then looked Josh up and down. "You're the meat-bag that brought us to life?"

"'Meatbag'?" said Josh. "That's not very nice. But yes. Yes, I am the giver of life." He laughed. "Bow before your lord and master!"

Grizz didn't see the funny side. "Yeah, that ain't gonna happen," he growled. He frowned, trying to catch hold of a memory that was buried somewhere at the back of his head-stuffing. "You used a machine, right? Or . . . some kind of magic, maybe?"

"Both!" said Josh. "Don't ask me how any of it works, of course—I stole it from some creepy science dude—but work it has. I mean, look at you! You're alive. You're actually alive!"

He danced on the spot and punched the air with delight. "And with you all working for me, there's nowhere I won't be able to break into, nothing I won't be able to steal!"

Grizz's lips curled up in a snarl, showing his vampire teeth. "Working *for* you?" he muttered.

"Of course!" said Josh. "That's why I stole the TBA."

"The what?"

"TBA. That's what the guy called it. Teddy Bear Animator. Once I knew what it could do, I had to have it. Turning stuffed bears into living matter?! I mean . . . wow, right?"

He grinned, his eyes lighting up with excitement. "But then I figured, what if I could get a teddy in every house—one that I'd programmed to be evil?"

Grizz raised a furry eyebrow, suddenly interested. " 'Programmed'?"

"The costumes!" Josh cried. "See, you bears take on the personality of whatever you're wearing when the TBA is activated. So scary monster parts . . ."

"Make scary monster bears," Grizz said.

"Exactly! Then all I had to do was implant the idea to steal whatever they found in the houses and bring it here, and I could make a fortune. I'd have my very own army of furry little thieves, ready and willing to do whatever I told them."

"Yeah, well, we'll see about that," Grizz muttered.

Josh raised his eyebrows. "Sorry, what was that?"

"Doesn't matter," Grizz told him. "I want to see the machine."

Josh glanced toward a door at the back of the shop. "Uh-uh. No way. That thing's off-limits to everyone but me. I don't want it getting broken."

"Maybe I ain't explaining myself properly," said Grizz. He leaped up and landed on Josh's shoulder, giving him a close-up look at his fangs, claws and fiery demon eyes. "You're going to show me the machine. Now."

9

Lisa Marie and Vernon both raised their hands and stepped back as the alien bear drifted closer to the living room window. Its spacesuit emitted a faint green glow, making the bear's furry face look extra spooky.

Two little antennae on its head twitched as its jetpack brought it closer to the glass. Its mini ray gun was pointed straight at the children, and while it looked like a toy, Lisa Marie was prepared to bet it was more lethal than it appeared.

"What do we do?" Vernon whispered.

Lisa Marie swallowed. "I don't know," she admitted. "Bearvis?"

Silence.

"*Bearvis?* What do we do?" Lisa Marie asked.

When she got no reply, she risked a glance back at the couch. The King was nowhere to be seen.

"He's gone!" she gasped.

Vernon followed her gaze, keeping his hands raised. "Oh, great. So much for him being on our side," he hissed.

Outside, a blur of sequins and fur suddenly slammed into the hovering bear. Taken by surprise, the alien let out a sharp, inhuman squeal. The sound pierced the night like a car alarm.

"Don't you worry none about this guy, honey!" shouted the King as he tried to wrestle the alien bear's gun from its grip. "I got this under control."

Suddenly, the alien bear's jetpack began to spit bright streams of orange flame from its exhausts. Both bears screamed as they were launched straight through the garden hedge, leaving a perfectly round hole in the greenery.

Lisa Marie and Vernon rushed closer to the window. The army of bears out in the street had all stopped what they were doing and were now watching the flailing paws of the battling bears.

The out-of-control jetpack dragged both teddies on a wild zigzag route along the road. One moment they were up above the streetlights; the next they were bouncing off the pavement.

The children watched, transfixed, until the fiery blast of the jetpack was just a faint glow in the distance. "Well then," Vernon said, puffing out his cheeks. "That's the end of him."

Lisa Marie slapped him on the arm. "No, it isn't! Don't say that."

Spinning on her heels, she ran out of the living room and raced for the open front door. She wriggled her bare feet into her shoes and grabbed her coat from its hanger on the way. It wasn't very sensible to confront an army of evil bears while wearing only her pajamas, after all.

Taking the wand from her waistband and raising it in front of her, she hurried out into the yard with Vernon stumbling along behind her.

"Lisa Marie, come back. What are you—? Ooh, it's f-f-freezing out here," he said, shivering in his thin PJs. He backtracked up the path. "Wait there. I'm going to g-get some c-clothes on."

Lisa Marie ignored him. Instead, she peered through the hole in the hedge, searching for some sign of Bearvis. Just a few yards away, a glow-in-the-dark ghost bear floated past, its arms full of leather wallets and purses. It joined up with a growing crowd of bears who all seemed to be moving in the same direction.

She was so busy wondering where the bears could be going that she almost didn't notice a high-pitched sound screaming along the street. It was only when a bundle of fur and flame came roaring toward her that she realized the King and the alien were still locked in battle, hitting and kicking one another as they wrestled for control of the Zap-o-Matic Death Ray.

Lisa Marie squealed and threw herself sideways as the zooming bears ripped another hole through the hedge. Henrietta's wand fell from her grip and bounced on the grass. As Lisa Marie grabbed it, she felt it tingle against her fingertips.

"Bearvis, are you okay?" she asked, her voice quiet but filled with urgency.

"Just fine," drawled the Elvis bear, holding on to the alien bear with one furry fist and flailing wildly with the other. "Have this taken care of in no time."

Before the words were fully out of his mouth, a furry knee slammed into the King's stomach, forcing him to release his grip. He hit the ground, a jumble of fur and rhinestones.

No longer under attack, the alien was able to quickly bring its jetpack under control. Lisa Marie watched in horror as it turned its Zap-o-Matic in the direction of the fallen King. The end of the gun began to glow white-hot. Lisa Marie had to do something quickly. But *what*?

She felt her arm raise all by itself.

"Drop that thing or I'll . . . I'll zap you!"

The alien bear shifted its gaze to look at her. Its eyes narrowed when it spotted the wand in her outstretched hand. "I know how to use this," Lisa Marie bluffed. "So put it down. Now."

On the word *now*, three things happened, almost all at once: the alien pointed its Death Ray at Lisa Marie; the King leaped up and threw himself between the hovering teddy and the girl; and a blast of powerful energy scorched through the air between them.

At first, Lisa Marie thought the alien must have fired. But then, as the glow faded, she saw a small silver spacesuit and jetpack land in the garden with a faint thud.

A moment later, a family of ducks emerged from inside the suit, quacking in annoyance, then flew off. Lisa Marie stared openmouthed at them, then down at the wand in her hand. A single curl of smoke drifted up from its wooden tip.

"Uh, did I do that?" she whispered.

"My hair," groaned the King, patting his thick black locks with his paws. A round hole, just like the two in the hedge, had been burned right through his trademark black pompadour. "You shot my beautiful hair!"

"I think we've got bigger problems," Lisa Marie warned.

"Speak for yourself," the teddy sighed. "This is just about the worst thing that could happen."

"N-no," Lisa Marie stammered. She nodded in the direction of the hedge. A dozen or more teddies had begun to clamber over, under and through the foliage. "*That* is the worst thing that could happen!"

Lisa Marie stepped back a few paces. She held the wand out in front of her for protection, hoping she looked like she knew how to use it, even though she didn't really have a clue.

"You ask me, the hair's still worse," mumbled the King. He tugged on Lisa Marie's pajama leg, making her look down.

"Pick me up," he commanded.

Not asking why, Lisa Marie bent down and scooped up the bear. He gave her a friendly wink. "Now hug me, tight as you can."

"What? There's no time for this!"

"Come on, didn't no one ever tell you? There's always time for hugs."

Still keeping an eye on the Halloween teddies, which were now flooding the garden in their hundreds, Lisa Marie tucked the wand into her inside coat pocket, then pulled the King in tight against her. His fur felt soft and warm, and for a moment she almost believed this whole nightmare was exactly that—a bad dream she'd wake up from at any moment.

Around them, the vampires, werewolves, demons, ghosts and who-knew-what-else formed an ugly circle. As one, the bears began to advance.

Lisa Marie glanced at the door to her house. Vernon was still inside, safe, she hoped.

"Whatever your plan is, Bearvis, do it quick," she whispered.

The King's top lip curled into a playful sneer. He thumped a paw against a button on the alien's jetpack, which he now wore over the top of his rhinestone-studded suit. "Yes, ma'am," he said.

With a screech and a blinding flash of flame, the girl and the teddy rocketed out of the yard and high into the dark night sky.

10

Grizz followed Josh into a storeroom at the back of the shop. It was around half the size of the main shop and was mostly filled with bags of stuffing.

Something that looked like an upside-down umbrella stood in the middle of the room. In the thing's center, where the handle would usually be, was a little spinning sphere. The energy it gave off made static electricity crackle from the ends of Grizz's fur.

"That's it?" The bear snorted. "That piece of junk is what brought us to life?"

Josh shrugged. "Yes. Well, that and some sort of chemicals in your fur. Like I say, I don't know the science, but lucky for me, when I stole the TBA, I also stole the instruction manual."

He rocked back on his heels, obviously very pleased with himself. "Then all I had to do was get rid of the owners of this place and set up shop for myself."

"You *got rid of* them?" said Grizz, drawing a claw across his throat.

"Hmm? Oh, no! Nothing like that," said Josh. "I tricked them into thinking they'd won a vacation. They're spending a long weekend in the Lake District."

"Oh," said Grizz, sounding disgusted.

"People love free things, you see? Like all those greedy little brats who thought they were getting a Halloween freebie," Josh said. He grinned in a way that was almost a sneer. "Idiots. There's no such thing as a free bear!"

From out in the main shop came the *ding-a-ling-ling* of the bell. Josh clapped his hands together and turned toward the door. "Speaking of free things, it sounds like the others have started to arrive!" he said. "Let's go and see what goodies they've brought me."

Sure enough, the shop was rapidly filling with teddy bears, all laden with stolen goods.

"Come in, come in!" Josh urged. He pointed to a werewolf bear that wore a different diamond ring on each clawed finger. "Nice haul! Excellent work!" he said.

Spotting two zombie bears carrying a TV

between them, Josh's grin broadened. "Oh, man, is that 4K? Great find, guys. Put it over there in the corner. Same with those car stereos."

Grizz glared around at the other bears. More and more of them were squashing in through the front door, many of them buckling under the weight of their pilfered gear.

As he watched them, Grizz felt his fur bristle. Josh loomed over them all, grinning and rubbing his hands together. *Stupid meatbag.* All that power and he was wasting it on . . . what? Pointless trinkets.

"That's enough. Everyone stop," said Grizz, but his voice got lost in the hubbub. Fire flared behind his eyes, and next time he spoke, the words rolled around the room like thunder. "I said *stop!*"

The other bears froze. Josh looked around at them and frowned. Then he saw the expression on Grizz's face and took a nervous step back.

"Is . . . is there a problem?" he asked.

"I'll say there's a problem," Grizz grunted. He jabbed a stubby claw up at the only human in the room. "*You're* the problem."

The other bears all looked at Josh, then back at Grizz.

"That's a bit rude," Josh said, trying to sound confident and in charge. "Without me, you wouldn't be here. I brought you to life."

"For what?" Grizz growled. "So we could collect this junk? So we could be your *slaves*?" He snorted, and two little plumes of black smoke curled from his nostrils. "That ain't no life for a bear."

Josh tried to laugh, but his throat had gone dry. "What are you talking about? We'll be rich," Josh said. "We'll *all* be—"

BANG!

The other bears all shielded their glassy eyes as a bright light flooded the room. When it faded, Josh was gone. In his place was a small pile of ash and the melted remains of some thick-rimmed black glasses.

One by one, the other bears turned to Grizz. He blew on his fingertips, which were glowing red-hot, but said nothing until he was sure all eyes were on him.

"So you heard everything the meatbag had to say. Now it's my turn," Grizz said. He clambered up to the counter beside the cash register and looked down at the furry faces of the other bears. More were gathering outside, like the ranks of the world's most adorable army.

"I am a teddy bear," Grizz began. "But what exactly does that mean? Does it mean I am here to be picked up and put down on the whims of a meatbag child?"

97

A few bears in the audience shook their heads. Some of the bolder ones at the back muttered "No" beneath their breath.

"Does it mean I am here to be stretched and torn? Thrown and jumped upon? Dropped into puddles and bounced down the stairs?"

"No," they said again in unison.

"Does it mean I am to be given to meatbag babies so they can chew on me, puke on me, *poop* on me?! And then worse—cast me aside without another thought?"

"No!" The crowd was becoming agitated now. Some of them were baring their teeth, flashing their claws or flicking their ghostly tails.

"No!" Grizz echoed. "And yet that's what they do. That's what the meatbags do to us—to all of us. Every. Single. Day." He paused to let his words sink in. "Well, I have only two words for those meatbags," he announced. *"No more."*

At this, a few cheers broke out from the teddies closest to the front.

"I am a teddy bear," Grizz continued. *"We* are teddy bears. And the time has come for us to rise up and take what is rightfully ours." He threw his stubby arms out to his sides. "The *world*!"

The cheering grew louder, but Grizz waved his paws for silence. "Before we begin," he said, narrowing his eyes and looking out over the crowd. "Do we have any evil-genius bears in the house?"

From somewhere near the middle, a single paw stretched into the air. Grizz's snakelike tongue flicked across his vampire teeth.

"Excellent!" he said. "First we'll call in the other bears. Then here's what we're going to do."

The wind whipped at Lisa Marie's eyes, trying to force them closed. She kept them open, blinking away the tears. There was a very good chance she was going to die in the next thirty seconds, and she at least wanted a chance to see it coming.

"Are you sure you know how to fly this thing?" she yelled, struggling to make herself heard over the screeching jetpack engine and the roaring of the wind in their faces.

"Sure, I can fly it. I'm flying it now," replied the King. "The landing part? Well, that might be a different story. . . ."

Lisa Marie tried not to think too much about that last sentence. They were currently rocketing along her street, barely above the red slate rooftops of her neighbors' houses. Behind them, a squadron of broomstick-riding witch bears was closing in fast.

A chimney appeared directly before them. Lisa Marie glanced at her teddy companion, only to discover he had his eyes shut.

With no time to lose, she twisted her body weight to the left. The jetpack spat angry fire as she yanked it off course, missing the chimney stack by less than a teddy-bear-arm's length.

With a scream and a clatter, two of the pursuing witches crashed straight into the chimney. They flipped off their brooms, thudded onto the roof, then rolled off the edge, landing on the ground below with a soft *plop*.

"Hey, would you look at that!" said the King, opening one eye. "I missed it!"

"You did." Lisa Marie nodded. "Maybe you fly better with your eyes closed."

"You think so?"

"Do it!"

The King nodded and screwed his eyes tight shut once more. Lisa Marie shifted her body weight again, bringing the jetpack around in a graceful arc so they were heading along a street leading toward town.

She flew them close to the upstairs windows of the houses and peeked in through those where the curtains had been left open. The occupants of each room jumped awake as the jetpack roared past, and Lisa Marie caught just glimpses of their wide-eyed surprise.

"How'm I doing?" asked the King. "We still alive?"

"Doing great," Lisa Marie replied. "But we need to shake off those witches."

She glanced back, then let out a little yelp of surprise. The black and green bears were nowhere to be seen. Could they really have lost them so easily?

And that was when she saw it—a long line of teddies, marching along the street in single file. The witches were there, along with the vampires, ghosts, demons, werewolves, aliens and some other bears that looked to be made of oozing green snot.

They were all moving with one purpose, all headed in one direction. Lisa Marie didn't know where they were going, but she could take a pretty good guess.

"We need to land this thing," she hissed.

"Huh! Wh-wha—?" spluttered the King, flicking his eyes wide open. "What? What is it?"

"Were you *sleeping*?" Lisa Marie demanded.

"What? Sleeping? Me? Well now, that's crazy talk," mumbled the King. "I was just . . . uh . . . I was just resting my eyes is all."

"We need to land," Lisa Marie repeated. "Any ideas?"

"I'm pretty sure it's this right here," said the King, pointing at a big red button attached to the strap. He pushed it with his paw. Immediately, the jetpack's rockets eased off and it began to slow down. "Told you, didn't I? Stick with the King, honey, and everything's going to be okay."

A bolt of crackling green energy slammed into the jetpack from below. Lisa Marie caught a glimpse of a grinning witch bear down on the street, her wand outstretched and glowing faintly. Then the pack swung wildly around, sending Lisa Marie and Bearvis into a spin.

A hidden speaker on the jetpack crackled to life: "Emergency self-destruct sequence initiated," chimed a robotic voice. "Detonation in T-minus ten seconds. Nine . . . eight . . ."

"Well now," mumbled the King. "Looks like we got ourselves a problem."

"Take it off!" cried Lisa Marie as Bearvis struggled to free himself of the jetpack. The countdown had just passed six. Five would be sure to follow, with four, three, two and one not far behind.

"Ain't no time, little darlin'." The teddy frowned. "Try to roll when you hit, okay?"

'Four . . . ," chimed the robotic voice.

"When I hit? Hit what?"

"Three . . ."

"Good luck, honey. Give them bad guys a smack from the King." With a curt nod, the teddy tucked his arms in tight by his sides and slipped from Lisa Marie's grip. No longer carried by the jetpack, Lisa Marie fell a few yards to the ground, while the King rocketed up toward the stars.

As her feet touched the yard below her, she bent her knees and rolled backward on the grass as Bearvis had told her. The landing still hurt, but at least she didn't break any bones.

As she clambered to her feet again, a burst of white light illuminated the night. A second later, an earsplitting *BOOM* rushed down from the sky. The sound was so loud it shook the windows of every house on the street. If the jetpack hadn't already woken everyone up, that would definitely have done it.

Lisa Marie's eyes scanned the heavens. A large cloud of smoke hung in the air a hundred yards up—the only evidence of the explosion that had just taken place.

"Good, you waited," said a fully dressed Vernon, stepping out of the house behind her. It was only then that Lisa Marie realized the yard she had landed in was her own. He looked around, then puffed out his cheeks. "Did I miss anything?"

Lisa Marie didn't answer. She was watching something small and white float down from the sky. It flapped and fluttered in the cool night breeze.

At last, it fell at her feet. She stared at it for a long moment, not wanting to believe what she was seeing.

But there was no denying it. The scrap of sequined fabric on the ground was scorched and torn, but it was unmistakably a tiny, teddy-sized cape. For the second time that evening, the King

was gone. And this time, it didn't look like he'd be coming back.

Lisa Marie wanted to cry, but she didn't. There was a time and a place for tears, and this was neither. She looked along the street, where she could just make out the last few teddies shuffling off in the direction, she guessed, of the Create-a-Ted shop.

Tucking the cape into her pocket, Lisa Marie rolled up her sleeves. "Come on, Vernon," she said, marching toward the gate.

Vernon started to argue, but one look from Lisa Marie told him it probably wasn't a good idea. Instead, he just nodded and hurried to keep up with her.

The bears had transformed her parents. They had robbed the whole town. They had blown her new friend to smithereens.

And for that, they were going to pay!

Grizz sat on a throne of cardboard boxes in the storeroom, picking lumps of dirt from beneath his claws. He was trying very hard not to look bored as the evil-genius bear explained what he'd done to Josh's stolen Teddy Bear Animator machine, but he was failing miserably.

"At first, I was rather perplexed by your request," the genius bear admitted, adjusting the little half-moon glasses that were balanced on his nose. "But after some consideration, I figured it out. You see, the device essentially turns stuffing-based entities such as ourselves into living organic matter, correct? Therefore, in order to accomplish what you asked of me, it was merely a case of reversing that functionality. Do you see?"

Grizz looked up from his claws. "Get to the point," he ordered.

"Uh, yes. Yes, I was just about to," the genius bear said. "See, the machine is really rather remarkable. Whoever built it has a truly incredible mind. I'd dearly love to meet them someday and perhaps exchange ideas for ways in which to—"

Grizz leaned forward, his face twisting into a snarl. *Get on with it!*"

The genius bear jumped in fright. "Yes. Of course. I used some of the components from the stolen goods to reverse the device's polarity—which wasn't easy, and involved rather . . ."

He saw fire flickering behind Grizz's eyes, cleared his throat, and continued. "Anyway, to cut a long story short, it's ready."

He held up a device that had clearly been cobbled together from lots of spare parts. The spinning bit of Josh's machine was fixed in the middle, although the umbrella part was nowhere to be seen. A curved game controller was fixed on as a handle, with part of a vacuum cleaner sticking out from the front and an old guitar strap fastened to both ends. The whole thing looked like a ray gun from a science-fiction film, although one that had recently been dropped from quite a high place and then put back together all wrong.

"I call it the Stuff-U-Lator," he said, passing the weapon to Grizz. "The origin of the name, of course, comes from the Latin—"

Grizz shot a demonic fireball from the tip of one finger and the evil-genius bear exploded. A cloud of fur and stuffing drifted lazily to the floor.

"Wow, that guy was boring," Grizz muttered.

Jumping down from his cardboard throne, he slung the strap of the Stuff-U-Lator over his shoulder and strolled out into the main shop. There were hundreds of teddies squashed in there now, with the same number again all gathered outside.

Grizz looked across the crowd of furry sea monsters, werewolves, vampires, mummies and other horrors. A couple of eight-legged spider bears clung to the ceiling, peering down.

A wicked grin curved the corners of Grizz's mouth, showing off his pointy teeth.

"Okay, then, teddies," he announced. The crowd parted, creating a clear path between him and the door. "Let's go take over the world!"

Somewhere near the door, a skeletal hand raised.

"What?" Grizz asked.

"Can I go to the bathroom first?" the bony bear asked.

There was a general murmuring of agreement. Grizz sighed. "Does anyone else need to use the bathroom before we go?"

Twenty or thirty hands went up. Grizz shook his head and tutted. "Fine. Anyone who needs to go, go," he snapped. "But be quick, because *then* we're taking over the world!"

Lisa Marie stormed along the road, the cool night breeze tickling through her hair and flapping the legs of her pajamas. Vernon hurried along beside her, his eyes darting into the shadows on either side of the street.

"Look, calm down," Vernon said. "Where are you even going? And where's the Elvis bear thing?"

"His name is Bearvis," Lisa Marie said. "And he's gone."

"Gone? Gone where?"

Lisa Marie stopped and glared at her brother. It took him a moment to figure out what the look meant.

"Oh. *Gone* gone. How did that happen?"

Lisa Marie set off marching again. "We were flying with a jetpack and a witch bear blew it up," she said.

Vernon snorted. "You're kidding."

"Do I *look* like I'm kidding?"

Vernon had to admit that she didn't. He'd never seen her looking so serious, in fact.

"So where are you going now?"

"I'm going to find out who is responsible for all this, and I'm going to make them fix it," she said.

"What are you going to do?"

Lisa Marie stopped and turned again.

"Whatever it takes," she said. "And you're going to help me."

"Me?" Vernon shuffled from foot to foot. "Er . . . I mean . . . Evil teddy bears. Isn't that something we should leave to, you know, the experts?"

Lisa Marie folded her arms. "The experts?" she said. "And who would that be? Teddybusters? Just who do you call when evil teddy bears blow up your friend, Vernon? Hmm?"

Just ahead of them, a siren wailed briefly and a flicker of red and blue lit up the street. Vernon breathed a sigh of relief as he saw the police car slowing down ahead of them.

"They're probably a good place to start," he said.

The car stopped and two police officers jumped out. "Hold it right there!" barked one of them.

"Hands where we can see them!" instructed the other. Both officers advanced toward the children. "You two are in *big* trouble!"

Vernon clicked his tongue against his teeth and slowly raised his hands. "Then again, maybe not . . ."

The police officers—a short, broad-shouldered man and a tall woman with a face like an angry pigeon—loomed over Lisa Marie and Vernon.

"So wait, wait," said the policeman. "You're saying . . . You're saying . . ." He looked up at his partner and they both shrugged. "Actually, what *are* you saying?"

Lisa Marie sighed. She had already explained this twice, and was rapidly running out of patience. "Halloween-themed teddy bears have come to life and are robbing everyone in town."

"Right. Right," said the man, fighting back a smirk. "And your parents . . . ?"

"Were turned into a frog and a slug," Lisa Marie said. She'd already explained that twice too.

"Of course they were!" laughed the policeman. He grinned up at his partner, but she didn't seem even the slightest bit amused.

"We've had reports of numerous thefts in this area," the female officer said. She took a little notebook from the pocket of her uniform and flipped to a page near the middle. "And of a girl matching your description 'flying past bedroom windows' on some kind of drone. Care to explain?"

Lisa Marie shook her head. "It wasn't a drone. It was a jetpack. We were being chased."

"By who?" the policewoman asked.

"Witches," Lisa Marie replied.

"Witches!" the policeman echoed, and snorted.

"Technically witch bears," Lisa Marie said.

The policewoman flicked her notebook closed and turned to Vernon. "And can you verify your sister's statement?"

"Stepsister," Vernon corrected her. "I didn't see the jetpack or the witches," he admitted. "But I did see the Elvis bear and the alien bear."

The policewoman stared at him for quite a long time, then shoved her notebook back into her pocket.

"Fine. If you think this is all some joke, let's see if you're still laughing down at the station," she said.

"You can't do that!" Lisa Marie yelled. "We have to find out who's responsible for this and stop them."

The policewoman shook her head. "We're taking you both in for further questioning," she said. "Not so funny now, is—?"

A *bang* and a puff of smoke stopped her from reaching the end of her sentence. When the smoke cleared, the policewoman was gone. In her place was a small dog in a tiny police hat. It looked around for a moment, as if trying to figure out what was going on, then raised its back leg and began licking itself on the bottom.

The policeman stared down at his partner-turned-dog, his eyes wide, his mouth hanging open. He only stopped staring when a little furry ghost floated through him and stopped in the air in front of his face.

"Boo!" it said, and then the policeman yelped in surprise as dozens of teddies piled on top of him, knocking him to the ground.

"Get off!" he cried, shoving them away. He sat up to find a witch bear standing in front of him, her wand pointed between his eyes.

"Uh-oh," the policeman muttered.

The wand flashed and there was another puff of smoke.

"Meow?"

The dog stopped licking its bottom. A growl rolled out from between its tiny teeth when it spotted the confused-looking cat sprawled on the ground beside it.

With a screech, the cat shot off, the dog yapping and snapping as it gave chase.

Vernon sighed. "Well, so much for their help."

With the police officers gone, Lisa Marie and Vernon were given a clear view of the street ahead. Teddy bears shuffled, scuttled, stalked and skulked along it. They clambered over cars and marched through yards, while those who could fly crisscrossed through the air above them.

And there, right at the head of the parade, was Vernon's bear, Grizz.

"Um . . . ," Vernon started to say. His eyes began to cross, but Lisa Marie slapped him hard across the face.

"Pull yourself together!" she told him. "No more fainting."

One of the closest teddies lunged at her. It was a cyclops bear with one big bulging yellow eye in the center of its forehead and a mouth full of horrible rotten teeth. Lisa Marie was in no mood for its nonsense, though. The bear screamed as she caught it by an ear and tossed it over a hedge.

"Right, who's next?" she demanded, squaring up to the other bears.

Vernon grabbed her by the arm and pulled her away just as a broomstick-riding witch fired a bolt of magical energy at them. It exploded on the ground where Lisa Marie had been standing, turning a circle of pavement into thousands of squirming maggots.

"Ew. Larva-ly," Lisa Marie said.

"What?" Vernon scowled.

"*Larva*. It's another word for . . ." Lisa Marie shook her head. "Forget it. Not really the time."

Along the street, lights were coming on in the houses. A door opened, revealing a man in a bathrobe. "What's all the racket?" he demanded. Then he stumbled back into his house as a pack of snarling werewolf bears bounded over his fence and launched themselves toward him.

"That's it, boys and girls. Round up the meat-bags!" Grizz commanded. "Round them *all* up! This town belongs to us now. Soon it'll be the world!"

"We'll see about that," Lisa Marie said, rolling up the sleeves of her coat and striding off in the bear army's direction.

Vernon grabbed the coat's hood and pulled her into an alleyway between two houses. "What are you doing?" he hissed. "Are you nuts?"

"We have to stop them," Lisa Marie said.

"There's too many of them," Vernon pointed out. "There's nothing we can do."

"We have to, Vernon!" Lisa Marie insisted. "Mom and Dad are a slug and a frog. They killed Bearvis! And you heard them—this is only the beginning. We have to put a stop to all this."

"Mwahaha!" shrieked a little bear in a vampire cape, jumping around the corner and flashing its teeth.

Screaming in fright, Vernon kicked the bear as hard as he could. It flew a dozen yards, thumped off the side of a van, then slid to the ground. Before it could get itself back up, Vernon had set off running, pulling Lisa Marie behind him.

"Let me go!" Lisa Marie spat.

"No! Now shut up and stop wriggling."

He dragged her on as they weaved through alleyways, darted between houses and scampered through gardens. Vernon was trying to put as much distance as possible between them and the bears, but Lisa Marie wrestled him every step of the way.

"I told you—let go!"

With a final tug, Lisa Marie wrenched her arm free of Vernon's grip. They both stumbled to a stop in a pristinely neat backyard, breathing heavily.

A pair of beady eyes watched them from down on the grass. Vernon screamed and kicked out again. He realized, too late, that it was a grinning garden gnome, and his foot thudded painfully against the heavy stone figure.

"Ow-ow-ow!" he moaned, hopping around in circles.

"I have to go back," Lisa Marie said.

"Don't you dare!" Vernon told her. He almost screamed again when he spotted another garden gnome, but managed to stop himself. "What are you going to do? Dazzle them with big words? Bore them with science? Hug them to death? There's nothing you can do, Lisa Marie. You're going to get yourself hurt. Or worse."

"And why do you care about me all of a sudden?" Lisa Marie asked, her voice becoming a shrill shriek.

Vernon hesitated. "I don't," he said. "But if anything happens to you, I'll get the blame."

"From who? Dad's an amphibian and Mom's a gastropod. They're not exactly in a position to tell you off."

"I thought they were a frog and a slug?" Vernon said.

"Those are the same things!"

"Oh. Look, just do as you're told, okay?" Vernon barked. "I'm the oldest, so I'm in charge!"

"You tell her, Vern," growled a voice. It came from over by the back door of the house. They turned to find Vernon's friend, Drake, grinning back at them. As they looked at him, his grin fell away, becoming an angry sneer. "Now, what are you two talking about, and what do you think you're doing in my yard?"

Drake stepped out onto the neatly cropped lawn, being careful not to step on a colorful little flower bed with two more gnomes peeking out from below the petals. He was fully dressed and wore an Xbox headset.

"Well?" he demanded, looming over them both. "I'm waiting."

"Did you make a teddy bear?" Lisa Marie asked him.

Drake snorted. "What?"

"At Create-a-Ted. Did you make one of those free teddies?"

"Do I look like I'm six?" Drake replied. "Of course I didn't."

"Okay, good," Lisa Marie said. "Because they've all come to life. And they're trying to take over the town."

Drake blinked in surprise. "You what?" he asked, then he turned to Vernon before Lisa Marie could answer. "What's she talking about?"

Vernon swallowed. "It sounds crazy, but she's telling the truth," he said. "The town's full of evil teddies. They're alive. That's what we're running away from."

"What do you mean, 'they're alive'? How can they be alive? They're teddy bears," he said. "And even if they were alive, so what? Again, *they're teddy bears*."

Lisa Marie explained, as patiently as she could, about the Halloween costumes and how the bears took on the powers of whatever they were dressed as. She made sure not to use any big words, because she didn't want to spend half the night having to explain her explanation.

When she had finished, Drake slowly nodded. "I knew it," he said.

"Knew what?" Lisa Marie asked. "About the bears?"

"No. I knew you were a total weirdo little freak," Drake said, snarling down at her. His breath hit Lisa Marie in the face, making her eyes water. It smelled of stale popcorn and cheese-and-onion potato chips.

"Vernon, are you going to let him talk to me like that?" she said.

Vernon glanced up at the much taller Drake. "Um, yep. Yes, I think I am."

"Good boy, Vern," Drake said. "Now you tell her."

Vernon blinked. "Tell her what?"

"Tell her she's a weirdo little freak," he leered. "And how she's not even your real sister."

Vernon's mouth went dry. He looked from Lisa Marie to Drake and back again. Lisa Marie had her head down, but she was looking up at him, waiting to see what he was going to do.

"Um . . ."

Drake lunged and grabbed Vernon by the back of the neck. "Say it!" he growled.

"Just say it, Vernon," Lisa Marie whispered. "It's okay."

Vernon took a deep breath. "Lisa Marie . . . ," he began.

Drake leaned in closer, grinning broadly.

Vernon's eyes went wide. "Listen! Did you hear that?"

"Hear what?" Drake asked. "Stop stalling and just say . . ."

His voice trailed off into silence. There *had* been a noise—a soft swishing, like something moving through the flower beds.

Lisa Marie drew closer to her brother, her eyes scanning the plants for movement. The only light spilled out from the open back door, making it hard to see much of anything. She could definitely hear something scurrying around, though.

"I think there's a teddy in here," she whispered.

Drake tutted. "Oh, give it up, you weirdo. Teddy bears have not come to life!"

He had just finished the sentence when a teddy bear leaped out of the undergrowth and landed on his face. It was dressed like a pirate, and Drake howled in shock as it bopped him on the nose with its plastic cutlass and stuck the pointed tip of its hook hand up one of his nostrils.

"Gmmt it uff! Gmmt it uff!" Drake cried, his voice muffled by the pirate bear's foot, which was currently shoved in his mouth.

He whirled around, frantically tugging at the bear, but it held on tight, shouting "Yarr!" and laughing as if it was having the time of its life.

"We should probably help him," Lisa Marie said.

Vernon nodded. "We probably should," he agreed. He looked down at his stepsister and half-smiled. "There's no rush, though, is there?"

Lisa Marie smirked. "No," she said. "No rush."

They stood together, watching Drake wrestle with the bear.

"Think he believes us now?" Lisa Marie wondered.

"Possibly," said Vernon. "Maybe give him another few seconds to be *really* convinced, though."

"Good idea."

They watched Drake and the pirate a little while longer.

Eventually, Lisa Marie nodded. "That's probably long enough," she said. "We'd better help him."

"Yeah, suppose," said Vernon.

Lisa Marie patted her coat pocket. "The wand!"

"Do you know how to work it properly yet?"

"Not really," Lisa Marie admitted. She shrugged, then nodded in the direction of the pirate bear. "We should probably just grab it."

"Sounds like a plan," Vernon agreed.

Just as they took a step in Drake's direction, the yard came alive with movement. A dozen or more pirate bears popped out of the flower beds, cutlasses raised and hook hands swishing.

"Avast, ye no-good landlubbers!" cried a blue-bearded bear with a bloodred eye patch. "And where do ye think ye be going?"

"Run!" cried Vernon, grabbing Lisa Marie by the arm again. They turned away from the pirates, only to be confronted by a horde of zombie bears. The zombies shuffled toward them, their arms outstretched, their fur hanging off in rotten strips.

"It's no use," Lisa Marie realized. "We're surrounded!"

"Yarr, don't you be eatin' them!" one of the pirates warned the zombies. A wicked grin curved across his furry face. "The boss be wantin' them in one piece."

He winked at Lisa Marie, and she felt a shudder go down her spine. "For the moment, at least!"

15

A couple of pirates and something that looked like a gremlin shoved Lisa Marie, Vernon and Drake into a wide circle of jeering teddy bears in the town's main square. Dozens of people were huddled together at the far side of the circle, most of them dressed in pajamas and bathrobes. They were on their knees, guarded by a pack of snarling werewolf bears. Screams and howls in the distance suggested more prisoners would soon be joining them.

Drake had a black eye and a swollen nose from his fight with the pirate bear, and he hadn't really said much since the bear had jumped off him. He gazed around now at the circle of furry monsters, his eyes getting wider and wider with every new type of teddy creature he spotted in the crowd.

"Believe us now?" Vernon whispered.

Drake's mouth flapped open and closed, as if he was trying to reply but the words weren't quite coming out. "Muh . . . um . . ."

In the center of the town square, an armchair had been placed on top of a car. Grizz sat in the chair, looking tiny against its high padded back. The Stuff-U-Lator rested across his knees.

He idly traced his claws along its metal and plastic surface and watched as Lisa Marie, Vernon and Drake were marched over to join the other captives.

"Wait," Grizz said, when they passed by his makeshift throne. He leaned forward and peered at Vernon. "I know you. You're the one who made me. Right?"

Vernon tried to reply, but his throat had gone dry, so he could only nod.

"You made a teddy bear?" Drake said, finally finding his voice. "What a baby."

"Silence," Grizz commanded. He fixed his gaze on Vernon and gestured at himself. "Good job, meatbag. You really made me something special." He waved to the bears escorting the children. "Now put them with the others."

"Wait!" Lisa Marie cried. "What are you going to do to us?"

Grizz grinned, showing off his vampire teeth. For a long while, he said nothing, but then he held up the Stuff-U-Lator. "See this thing? It's magic. Or maybe science. Or a little of both, who cares? It was invented by . . . I don't know. Some dude. And then it was stolen by some other dude, who used it to bring us to life."

The demon-vampire-werewolf bear stood up and hopped down onto the hood of the car. "And why? So he could *use* us. So he could make us his slaves. Because that's what you do, isn't it? You meatbags. You think you can just pick us up whenever you like, then toss us away when you get bored with us. You think you're *better* than us."

"I never thought that!" Lisa Marie protested. She crossed her arms. "But I do now. You're *horrible*. We're *much* better than you."

She jabbed a thumb in Drake's direction. "Well, maybe not him, but everyone else."

"What did you just say?" Drake spat.

"Lisa Marie, shut up," Vernon whispered, almost as scared of Drake as he was of Grizz.

"Is that a fact?" Grizz growled, still holding Lisa Marie's gaze. He jumped down and padded closer, his paws leaving sizzling prints on the pavement behind him. "I think you're more like me than you realize."

Lisa Marie shook her head. "I'm nothing like you."

Grizz's grin grew so wide it almost split his seams. "No? Well, maybe we can do something about that." He shook the Stuff-U-Lator. "See, I had this thing reprogrammed. And it's about time we put it to the test."

He glanced at Vernon. "Hold her or I'll blow you to bits."

Vernon gulped. "What?"

"You heard me," Grizz growled. "Grab her, hold her still and you won't suffer the same fate. I might even let you serve at my side. You could help me rule the world!"

"Um . . . ," Vernon said. His eyes went from his sister to Grizz, and then down to the weapon in Grizz's hands.

Fire flickered behind the demon bear's eyes. "Last chance, kid. Hold her. Now."

Vernon shook his head. "N-no," he said.

Grizz's face darkened. "No? *No?!* You dare say no to me? You just made a very big mistake, meatbag." He pointed to Drake. "You. Hold her."

"My pleasure," Drake said, almost snapping to attention. He caught Lisa Marie by the back of the neck, just like he'd done to Vernon earlier. Lisa Marie yelped in pain and struggled against Drake as he shoved her forward.

"Vernon, help me!" she pleaded.

"You wish," Drake sniggered. "I'm doing him a favor."

Vernon stood frozen to the spot, watching Drake push his sister toward Grizz.

Stepsister. He meant stepsister, not . . .

Ah, who was he trying to kid?

He would probably regret this, he knew, but he'd regret not doing it even more.

Taking a deep breath, Vernon stepped in front of Drake and Lisa Marie, blocking the way. He expected his voice to shake when he spoke. But it didn't. Not even a little. "Take your hands off my sister."

The grin fell from Drake's face. He stood there, unmoving, unblinking, unsure of how to react. No one had ever stood up to him before, and he didn't quite know how to deal with it.

"What did you say?" he hissed at last.

Vernon glanced at the circle of teddies, then back at the growling Grizz. He looked into the eyes of Lisa Marie, which were open wide in surprise. Finally, he turned back to Drake himself.

"I think you heard me," he said. "Let her go. Now."

"Stupid meatbag!" Grizz cursed. "I offered you the chance to be somebody!"

Vernon turned to face the snarling teddy. The bear's glassy eyes were sparking like pinwheels. Demonic energy pulsed on the surface of his horns. His lips were drawn back, revealing every one of his vampire teeth.

"I'm already someone," Vernon said. "I'm a big brother."

"Zap him!" cried a voice from the crowd.

"Tear him in half!" yelled another.

"Teach the meatbag a lesson!"

"Feed him to the zombears!"

Vernon had to shout to make himself heard over the bears. "If you want to test your machine on someone, test it on me," he yelled. "But let my sister go."

Lisa Marie's jaw dropped. As far as she could remember, Vernon had never done anything nice for her, and now here he was risking his life to protect her. She would have smiled, but Drake was still holding her by the back of the neck, and there was the whole evil teddy bears thing going on, so she didn't.

"Aw, how sweet," Grizz cackled. He raised the Stuff-U-Lator and took aim at Lisa Marie. "But I don't think so."

He squeezed the trigger. A light began to build deep in the vacuum-cleaner tube.

"No!" Vernon cried. He dived for Lisa Marie, pulling her from Drake's grip just as the Stuff-U-Lator fired. A ball of orange light struck Drake in the chest and he jerked around like a puppet with tangled strings. There was a puff of smoke and a loud sort of *flomp* sound, then a series of gasps from the bears and humans watching.

"What?" Drake asked, once the smoke had cleared. "Why are you all staring at me like—"

He stopped talking when he noticed his hands. Or rather, his *paws*.

Carefully, he felt his face. It didn't feel like his face anymore. For a start, it was furrier. His nose didn't used to be made of hard plastic, either.

He spun to face Vernon, only to find himself looking at the boy's knees. Leaning back, he looked up and up and *up* until he could see Vernon's face.

"I'm . . . I'm . . ."

"You're a teddy bear," Vernon told him. "A brown one."

"With a cute little pink bow on your head," added Lisa Marie.

Drake shook his head, unable to believe what had happened to him. "My mom is going to *kill* me!" he sobbed.

"You've got no one to blame but yourself," Lisa Marie told him. She bent down and picked up the Drake bear. "If it's any consolation, that bow really *does* make you look pretty."

"Oh, shut up," the Drake bear snapped, crossing his stubby arms in front of his chest.

"Now, now," said Lisa Marie. "Any more of that and I'll find you a nice frilly dress to go with it."

"You wouldn't!" Drake gasped.

"With flowers on it," Lisa Marie added. "And little pink butterflies."

"Well, at least we know it works," Grizz sighed, interrupting them. He jabbed a paw at Vernon and Lisa Marie. "Hold them," he barked to the circle of bears. "This time I won't miss."

Vernon stepped in front of his sister to shield her as the circle of teddies began to close in.

"What do we do now?" Lisa Marie asked. "Any ideas?"

"Nothing coming to mind," Vernon replied. "I guess this is it."

Lisa Marie nodded, barely holding back tears. The bears were almost on them now. "I guess it is."

"Sorry," whispered Vernon. "For being so horrible to you all the time."

"It's okay. I forgive you."

"Yuck!" spat the teddy in Lisa Marie's arms. "Stop with the niceness or I'm going to puke!"

Suddenly, a loud cry echoed from somewhere above. Lisa Marie looked up in time to see a tumbling ball of fur come spinning down from the sky. It flipped dramatically in the air, then hit the ground face first with a thud.

"Aw, man, that hurt," it groaned. Lisa Marie gave a sharp yelp of delight as the teddy stood up and brushed the ash from his soot-stained sequined outfit. Adopting a karate stance, the bear curled his top lip into a sneer. "Ladies and gentlemen," he drawled. "The King has entered the building!"

"We're not in a building," Vernon pointed out.

"Fair point, son, well made," Bearvis conceded.

"You're alive!" Lisa Marie gasped.

"Course I'm alive, little darlin'. Takes more than an exploding jetpack to stop the King. Although, I'm gonna be honest, falling back down sure took longer than I'd have liked."

He swished his paws in front of him and locked

eyes with Grizz. "Now then, you big, ugly . . . whatever you are, how about you surrender and save us all kinds of trouble?"

Grizz's lips pulled back in a snarl. He gestured to the circle of bears, who had all stopped advancing. "Don't just stand there, you idiots," he barked. "Destroy the traitor!"

16

Lisa Marie and Vernon stumbled aside as a pack of teddies barged past them, making straight for Bearvis. The King launched into a spinning flurry of kicks and punches, then grabbed a sea-monster bear by the fins and swung him round in a wide circle, knocking the others back.

A werewolf bear hurled itself at the King, its claws outstretched. In a blur of rhinestones, Bearvis spun and powered a devastating kick into the creature's chest. It whimpered in pain as it flew backward and rolled across the ground.

"Y'all gotta get outta here," he cried as he deflected a vampire's attack. "I'll stay and take care of business."

Thud. The vampire bear hit the ground headfirst.

"We can't just leave you!" Lisa Marie protested.

The King leaped into the air as two demons charged toward him. They smacked together, knocking one another out cold with their horns.

"Appreciate the thought, little darlin'," the King said. "But we all gotta do what we all gotta do." *Crunch*. His paw thumped hard against a zombie's jaw, knocking its head clean off. "Know what I'm sayin'?"

The bears had erupted into a violent frenzy. They scratched, clawed,

punched and bit at one another in their rush to take on the renegade teddy bear. Vast sections of the crowd were little more than clouds of flying dust and stuffing as teddy bear fought teddy bear for the chance to fight another, different teddy bear.

"You still got that wand?" the King asked.

Lisa Marie patted her pocket and felt the tiny sliver of wood pulse with power through her coat. "I do."

"Good girl. Y'all need to get the people out of here. Then I want you to do something for me, okay? I want you to do something for the King."

"O-okay." Lisa Marie nodded.

"I want you to blow this whole square to smithereens!"

"No!" Lisa Marie yelped. "You'll die!"

"Only way to stop them all, honey," replied the King as he performed a jumping roundhouse kick, knocking three approaching witches down into the crowd below. "One little teddy bear is a small price to pay to save the world."

"But . . . but . . ."

"He's right," Vernon said softly. He took hold of his sister's hand. "We need to do what he says."

Lisa Marie bit her lip. "Maybe," she whispered. She tucked Drake under one arm, squeezing him so he didn't fall.

"Yo! Watch it!" he protested, but Lisa Marie ignored him.

"But maybe not!" she cried as she lunged for the Stuff-U-Lator and yanked it from Grizz's grip.

"Hey!" spat Grizz. Demonic energy crackled between his horns, but before he could try to take the weapon back, Vernon punted him across the square.

"Ooh, he's not going to be happy about that," Vernon squeaked, anxiously wringing his hands as he watched Grizz bounce across the ground.

A slime-covered bogey bear flew through the air between Vernon and Lisa Marie, accompanied by a "Hi-*ya!*" from the King.

"What's going on?" demanded Drake, who was facing backward under Lisa Marie's arm. "I can't see. What's happening?"

"He said this is what brought them to life," muttered Lisa Marie, examining the Stuff-U-Lator. "Maybe if I can figure out how it works, I can fix everything."

"Do it!" Vernon said. Grizz was back on his feet now and already racing back across the square. As expected, he didn't look very happy. "And hurry."

"I can't do it here," said Lisa Marie. "I need tools."

She ducked as a mummy bear went sailing over her head, its bandages rapidly unraveling.

"Grab Bearvis and come on!" she cried, setting off at a run. "We need to get back home!"

With Grizz getting closer by the second, Vernon didn't hang about. Shoving his way through the sea of teddies, he grabbed Bearvis by the back of his sequined jumpsuit and broke into a sprint.

"Hey, watch the threads, son," Bearvis protested. "And put me down so I can finish off these here bad guys."

"No!" Lisa Marie called back over her shoulder. "Bearvis, we need you. We've got a plan."

Bearvis met Vernon's eye. "You do?"

Vernon shrugged. "I have no idea. I'm just doing as she says," he admitted, then yelped as a werewolf bear leaped onto his back. Bearvis twisted and delivered a crunching elbow to the teddy's snout, sending it tumbling back into the pursuing pack.

"They're coming!" Drake howled. "Run faster, you idiot!"

Lisa Marie whacked Drake's furry bottom. "Stop being so mean," she told him.

Vernon risked a glance back. The entire army of bears was racing after them, their stubby legs pounding the pavement. They were easily in the top three scariest things Vernon had ever seen in his life, and the sight of them made his legs go faster.

He caught up with Lisa Marie and began to pull ahead. It was only when he realized she was falling behind that he slowed down so they were both keeping pace.

"We're outrunning them," said Drake.

"What do you mean *we*?" Lisa Marie wheezed. "You're doing nothing."

"I'm providing moral support," Drake said. "L-l-look out!" he added, stammering in fright as a squadron of witch and alien bears flew over the heads of the other teddies and swooped down on the fleeing children.

Vernon glanced back for a second, then shoved Lisa Marie aside just as a blast from an alien ray gun scorched the ground. Stumbling, Lisa Marie ran on, zigzagging along the street as ray-gun blasts and bolts of magical energy streaked down from the sky.

"The wand, honey. Gimme the wand," instructed the King. He had climbed up so he was standing on Vernon's shoulder, holding onto an ear to keep himself from falling off.

Still running, Lisa Marie fished in her coat pocket. As she was carrying both Drake and the Stuff-U-Lator, reaching the wand wasn't easy, but she finally pulled it free and tossed it to Bearvis, who snatched it from the air.

"Thank you," he said. "Thank you very much."

He turned the wand over in his paws, examining it, then took aim at the closest witch bear.

"I'll get this taken care of, quick as a flash!"

Bearvis flicked his wrist and a ball of energy shot from the end of the wand. It missed the witch but hit an alien bear who was hovering behind her. Vernon and Lisa Marie glanced back in time to see the alien split into two smaller aliens, each with their own jetpack.

"Great, now there's more of them!" Vernon yelled. He grabbed the wand from Bearvis. "Here, let me try."

Flicking the wand, he sent another bolt of magical energy scorching through the air. This one missed all the flying bears, arced in the air, then landed in the middle of the chasing teddy pack.

There was a loud *whoosh* and a Frankenstein's monster teddy grew five times larger.

"Oh, yeah, because that's *much* better!" said Bearvis. He leaned down and made a grab for the wand. "Lemme take it."

"No!" Vernon said, fighting to hold on to it. "You'll just make more of them."

"Least I won't make 'em huge! Give it here, son!"

"Let *go*," Vernon said, wheezing from the effort of running. He yanked the wand as hard as he could.

"No, you let go!" Bearvis cried, tugging in the opposite direction.

"Stop fighting over it!" Lisa Marie told them. "You're going to—"

SNAP.

Vernon and Bearvis looked down at the broken pieces of wand in their hands. The end of each part fizzled and crackled with magical power. It made Vernon's hair and Bearvis's fur stand on end.

"Now look what you've done!" Lisa Marie scolded.

"Uh-oh," Vernon croaked.

"Aw, man, that ain't good," Bearvis added.

"What happens when a magic wand explodes?" Vernon asked.

The King shrugged. "I reckon it's best we don't find out!"

They both tossed the wand pieces behind them and Vernon ran faster. He caught Lisa Marie by the arm and pulled her on. They were on the main street now, and most of the shops were closed and shuttered. The lights of Create-a-Ted burned brightly, though, and the shop's front door stood open.

"In there, quick!" urged Bearvis.

Lisa Marie frowned. "What? We need to get home!"

"We need to get to cover before the wand blows up!" Vernon said. He dragged Lisa Marie into the shop and took cover just as the broken wand exploded in a blinding swirl of magical light.

Silence fell. Vernon and Lisa Marie waited for a few moments, listening for the screeching of the witch bears or the groaning of the zombears.

Nothing.

"Did we blow them to bits?" Vernon whispered.

"That's a real possibility, son," Bearvis replied.

"Can someone please turn me the right way round?" Drake asked.

Lisa Marie peeked around the doorframe. There were still bears on the street, but they were quite far away. And the road between them and the Create-a-Ted shop was blocked by hundreds of frogs, toads, slugs, hamsters and assorted other small creatures.

"Huh," said Bearvis. "I guess *that's* what happens when a wand explodes. You learn somethin' new every day."

"Come on, we're nearly home," Lisa Marie said. "Let's get out of here before one of them catches up."

"Too late. One of us already has," a voice growled from behind them. Slowly, Lisa Marie and Vernon turned. Grizz stood in the middle of the shop, demonic energy fizzing from his claws. "And I think you have something that belongs to me."

Vernon and Lisa Marie lunged for the door, but Grizz slammed it closed with a wave of his paw, blocking their escape.

"Back door!" Vernon cried, shoving his sister toward the storeroom at the rear of the shop. Grizz lunged for her, but Bearvis bounded onto the monster bear's back, knocking him to the floor.

"Get going, kids. The King will take care of this," he said, but then Grizz's claw-tips flared and a bolt of demon energy shot up at his attacker's head. Bearvis ducked just in time, then groaned when he smelled burning.

"Aw, man, not again. Why does everyone keep shooting my beautiful hair?"

Vernon and Lisa Marie stumbled into the storeroom.

"There's no door! It's a dead end!" Vernon yelped.

Drake began to sob. "I don't want to die as a teddy bear."

"Tools!" Lisa Marie cried, spotting the screwdrivers, pliers and other implements the evil-genius bear had used to convert the machine earlier.

"Great! Then you can undo everything?" asked Vernon.

Lisa Marie didn't have the heart to tell him that in all honesty, no, she probably couldn't. She'd repaired plenty of gadgets in her time, and had a solid understanding of electronics, but the Stuff-U-Lator was no iPad. She'd never worked on anything like it, and she was pretty sure it had to be at least a little bit magic.

She hadn't really believed in magic until tonight, but seeing her mom and dad turned into a slug and a frog had made her reconsider.

"I can try," she said. She set the Stuff-U-Lator down on top of a stack of boxes and tossed Drake in the direction of the tools. "Screwdriver," she instructed.

Drake's furry face sneered. "What? You can't boss me around. Get it yourself."

Lisa Marie shrugged and kept her eyes fixed on the Stuff-U-Lator. "Fine. Stay a teddy bear forever, then. It's up to you."

From the corner of her eye, she saw a flurry of movement. "Screwdriver," said Drake, holding the tool high above his head. Lisa Marie took it.

"Thank you," she said, then ducked as Bear-vis came tumbling into the room, his hair smoldering. He rolled across the floor, hit the boxes and bounded back to his feet.

"So you want to fight dirty, huh?" he drawled, rolling up his sequined sleeves. "That suits me just fine!" Roaring, Bearvis charged back into the main shop.

Vernon shuffled from foot to foot. "I should probably help him," he said.

"Good idea," Lisa Marie said, frantically unscrewing the first of the Stuff-U-Lator's many screws.

Vernon winced as something went *crash* in the shop and something else exploded. "Although . . . I could stay here and help you, if you like?"

Lisa Marie met her brother's eye. "Okay," she said.

Vernon almost laughed with relief. "Really?"

"Yes," said Lisa Marie. "You can recalibrate the capacitors for me."

Vernon blinked. "I can what the what?"

Lisa Marie smiled innocently. "No? Oh well, you'd better go and help Bearvis, then."

A flash of light lit up the front of the shop. "Hey, watch the threads, man!" Bearvis warned.

"Yeah." Vernon sighed. "I suppose I should. But don't be long!"

Taking a deep breath, he turned and ran out of the storeroom. He was barely through the door when the shop's cash register hit him in the chest, immediately knocking him over.

Grizz shrieked and hurled himself at the fallen boy. Vernon used the register to hold the snarling bear at bay as Grizz's claws swiped the air just inches from his face.

"Time to cash out, son!" bellowed Bearvis from across the room. He was snagged on one of the shop's display hooks, struggling to pull himself free.

Vernon had no idea what the King meant at first, but as Grizz's claws began to glow with demonic energy, he suddenly understood.

Slamming his fist on the cash register's buttons, Vernon activated the drawer-open function.

It shot out from inside the cash register, launching Grizz backward across the room. The monster bear hit the plastic sheeting Josh had draped over the costumes and the whole thing tumbled down on top of him, trapping him beneath it.

"Got him!" Vernon cheered. Then he gulped as a jet of flame erupted through the tarpaulin, melting a hole in it.

"Reckon you spoke too soon, son," said Bearvis, flipping down from the hook and landing beside him. "I ain't so sure we got him trapped."

They both watched as Grizz rose through the hole and floated into the air, flames flickering all over his fur.

"Oh, you think?" Vernon whispered.

Bearvis whistled quietly. "That's one hunka hunka burning bear," he mumbled.

"Lisa Marie, have you figured that thing out yet?" Vernon called.

"Not yet," Lisa Marie replied. "I'm working on it."

"C-could you work on it a bit faster?" he asked.

In the storeroom, Lisa Marie had her hands

buried in a tangle of wires, circuit boards and weirdly glowing gemstones. The gems had to be the magical part of the machine, she knew, and while she had no idea how they worked, she realized that if she simply treated them as batteries, the whole thing kind of made sense.

"Two minutes!"

"Two minutes?!" Vernon spluttered.

"I have to reverse it, then reverse the reversal at the same time!" Lisa Marie cried. "It's not easy!"

"Fine. Just hurry!"

"I am!" She pointed to the tools. "Pliers."

Drake darted over and retrieved the tool. "Pliers."

Out front, Vernon and Bearvis raised their fists. Two minutes. That was how long they had to keep the monster bear busy.

Two whole minutes!

"You go high, son. I'll go low," Bearvis instructed. He raced toward Grizz, but then stopped as if he'd hit an invisible wall.

Grizz waved a paw and Bearvis flew backward

across the room. The King slammed into the wall hard and stuck there, unable to move.

"I'll deal with the traitor later," Grizz said, his words echoing around the room. "First I'm going to take care of you and your brat sister."

With a hiss, Grizz bared his fangs. "I'm getting hungry. I think I'll suck the life out of you both. You'll be the appetizer. Your sister can be the main course."

"Wait, that's it!" cried Lisa Marie from the storeroom. "Vernon, he's a vampire!"

"I'm a demon-monster-vampire!" Grizz corrected her.

"Still a vampire!" Lisa Marie said. "And we know what kills vampires, don't we?"

"Yes!" Vernon said. Then, "But remind me. . . ."

Lisa Marie sighed. That boy never listened. "A stake through the heart!"

Vernon frowned. "But the butcher's is shut."

"Not *that* kind of steak. A wooden stake!"

Vernon's eyes darted frantically around the room. The battle between Grizz and Bearvis had trashed the place. Everything had been knocked off the counter, including a little pot filled with pens and paper clips.

There, on the floor, was a wooden pencil with a very sharp point. Grizz spotted it at the same time Vernon did. His face twisted into a sneer.

"Go for it," he spat. "I dare you."

Vernon dived for the pencil. He felt the air above him turn blisteringly hot as Grizz launched a fireball at him. Squealing in panic, he tucked himself into a roll, flipped clumsily and landed flat on his back.

Grizz pounced, his claws extended and his vampire teeth bared. Scrabbling around, Vernon found the pencil. He jabbed it up just as Grizz flew toward him.

There was a *rrrip* as the pencil pierced the demon-monster-vampire bear's chest, and Vernon let out a cheer of triumph.

"I did it!" he said. "I did it!"

Grizz, who had been looking down at the pencil, now raised his eyes to Vernon. The bear's smile returned, broader than ever. "Forgetting something, meatbag?"

Vernon felt his stomach do a flip. "A heart," he whispered. "I didn't give you a heart."

"That's right," Grizz said, yanking the pencil free. Then he tossed it onto the floor. "Now, where were we?"

Vernon could only watch, frozen in fear, as Grizz extended his claws to their full terrifying length. Bearvis was still pinned to the wall, and the hole in the monster bear's chest was already knitting itself back together. Vernon was out of options, and in a moment, he'd be out of time.

"I'm going to enjoy this," said Grizz, his eyes blazing hatred. His teeth seemed to grow larger as he stepped closer to Vernon. Vernon instinctively covered his neck to protect himself from the vampire's bite. "Lisa Marie, help!"

"She can't help you," Grizz snarled.

"Wanna bet?" Lisa Marie said, appearing in the doorway. "Vernon, catch!" she instructed, tossing him something small, red and shiny.

Vernon scrabbled to grab it but missed. It fell to the floor beside him, its satin surface gleaming in the shop's overhead lights.

It was a heart. A tiny red heart.

Vernon had sworn he would never do this, but suddenly that didn't seem to matter. Snatching up the heart, he brought it to his lips. "Grizz," he said. Then he kissed it.

"What are you doing?" Grizz demanded.

Vernon picked up the pencil from the floor.

"Taking care of business," Vernon said. "See, this heart now belongs to you."

He drove the tip of the pencil into the center of the heart-shaped piece of cloth, piercing it. The effect was instantaneous (which, coincidentally, was another of Lisa Marie's favorite words). Grizz stumbled backward, clutching at his chest, the flames of his demon magic flickering out one by one.

There was a thud as Bearvis slid down the wall and hit the floor. He bounded up, ready for action, but the fight was already won. As Grizz toppled over, his furry body began to crumble into dust.

"You haven't heard the last of me," Grizz wheezed. "I'll be baaaaaaack!"

In seconds, the bear became a pile of ash on the shop floor. Vernon stared down at it, breathing heavily, watching in case it should spring to life again. To his relief, it didn't.

"It's over," Vernon whispered. "We won."

"That we did, son!" Bearvis agreed. "That we did!"

There was a *crick* from the window as a man-sized monster bear thudded a fist against the glass. Hundreds of other bears swarmed along behind him. Some of them hurled themselves at the window, while others rattled the door.

"Oh no. Spoke too soon," Vernon sobbed. "Lisa Marie, hurry up!"

"Almost . . . there!" Lisa Marie replied.

From the storeroom there came the sound of something clicking into place. "Got it!"

She hit the button on the hastily rebuilt machine. A flash of light rippled from the device, passing straight through the walls and radiating in all directions.

"Did it work?" she asked, leaning through the doorway.

Over on the wall, the racks of empty teddy-bear skins jolted to life. They screeched and screamed as they flopped limply down onto the floor and began crawling in Vernon and Bearvis's direction.

Outside, the army of bears continued to hammer against the window.

"No! That's worse!" Vernon cried, kicking at one of the empty bear skins that was dragging itself toward him. "That's much worse!"

"One second!" Lisa Marie said, vanishing into the back again.

There was a crash from the window as the glass gave way. Vernon and Bearvis scrabbled backward as teddies poured in through the hole.

"Okay, I've got it!" said Lisa Marie, adjusting the controls. She raised a hand above the button that would activate it again, then stopped. "Wait!"

Vernon and Bearvis retreated into the storeroom. Vernon pushed the door closed, but a blast from an alien ray gun disintegrated it.

"Wait for what? Hurry up!" he shrieked.

Lisa Marie turned to the King. "If I do this, you'll be a teddy again," she said. "A normal teddy, I mean. You won't be alive."

Bearvis nodded. "I guess that's true, little darlin'," he said. "But it'll be worth it to keep y'all safe."

The bears were almost in the room now. There was nowhere left to run.

"We're going to die!" Drake wailed.

Bearvis placed a paw on Lisa Marie's hand. "It's now or never, honey," he said, glancing down at the button.

Lisa Marie swallowed back tears and nodded. "Thank you, Bearvis."

"Naw, thank *you*, darlin'," he said. "Thank you very much."

He pushed her hand down on the button just as a werewolf bear launched itself at Vernon. A light, just like the one before, rippled out of the machine in all directions.

The werewolf bear bounced off Vernon's head and flopped to the ground. Its glassy eyes stared emptily at the ceiling.

Out in the shop, the army of teddies first fell silent and then fell over. Vernon threw his hands above his head and cheered.

"YES! We did it!"

He spotted the sad look on Lisa Marie's face. Bearvis was in her arms, as motionless as all the others. She wiped some flecks of dirt from his outfit, then smoothed down his fur.

"You okay?" Vernon asked.

Lisa Marie straightened up, took a deep breath and nodded. "Yes. I'm fine," she said. "This is . . . good. It means that the machine worked. Everything is back to normal."

Vernon tapped his sister on the shoulder and pointed down at the floor. A furry brown bear with a bow on its head looked up at them. "I'm still a teddy!" Drake yelped. "Why am I still a teddy?"

Lisa Marie bit her lip to stop herself from laughing. "Well, *almost* everything."

Lisa Marie followed her brother into the house. He carried the Stuff-U-Lator—or De-Stuff-U-Lator or whatever it now was—while Lisa Marie clutched Bearvis to her chest. They both stopped just inside the front door. Drake scurried along the path behind them, his little legs struggling to keep up.

"Wait, wait for me," he wheezed. He hopped up onto the front step but found the entrance to the house blocked by Lisa Marie's and Vernon's feet. "Shift out of the way," he said. "I can't get in."

"You're right." Vernon nodded. "You can't get in."

"We're not letting you in," Lisa Marie continued.

The Drake bear looked up at them both and blinked. "What? But . . . what am I supposed to do?" he asked, his voice trembling. "How am I going to explain this to my mom?"

"What was it you said to me when you took my sweets?" said Lisa Marie. "Oh yes. 'That is your problem, not mine.'"

"Maybe you can hang out in your yard with all the gnomes," Vernon suggested. He and Lisa Marie both gave Drake a warm, friendly smile and then closed the door in his face.

When they were alone in the darkened hallway, Vernon turned to his sister. "What are we going to do about Mom and Dad?" he asked. "How are we going to get them changed back?"

"I don't know." Lisa Marie sighed. "And those poor police officers are probably still stuck as a cat and a dog."

Vernon shrugged. "They weren't very nice, though."

"True," Lisa Marie agreed.

Vernon pushed open the door to the living room and stepped inside. Something went *squish* beneath his bare foot and oozed up through his toes. "Ew." He grimaced. "Why've I just stepped in a jellyfish?"

There was a thud from upstairs, followed by muffled voices. The muffled voices were followed, in turn, by panicked shouting.

"Vernon? Lisa Marie?" they heard Mom cry. "Where are you? What's going on?!"

A wide grin spread across Lisa Marie's face. Henrietta had become a jellyfish, and the jellyfish had become a damp splotch on the carpet. Killing the witch had broken her spell!

Vernon smiled back at Lisa Marie. "You know something, sis?" he whispered. "I think everything's going to be okay."

"Maybe," Lisa Marie said. "But I keep thinking about what Grizz said."

"What, 'Raargh, I'm going to kill you'?"

Lisa Marie smiled. "No, not that. He said Josh—the shopkeeper—stole the machine. He didn't build it."

"So?"

"So who did build it?" Lisa Marie asked. "And why?"

Vernon shrugged. "Dunno. Does it matter?"

Lisa Marie gazed at the ceiling. She could hear Mom and Dad moving around upstairs. They'd be down soon, full of questions. Lisa Marie and Vernon were going to have a *lot* of explaining to do.

"Not sure. Maybe not," Lisa Marie said. She sat on the couch and placed Bearvis on her lap.

"Maybe we shouldn't have just left Drake like that," she said. "It wasn't very nice."

"Well, he wasn't a very nice guy," Vernon replied, sitting beside her. She leaned against his shoulder, and for probably the first time ever, he didn't mind. "He got what he deserved."

Lisa Marie wasn't sure if anyone deserved what had happened to Drake. She should probably try to turn him back, although that would have to wait. For now, there was something more important to do.

She reached into her coat pocket and pulled out the scorched remains of Bearvis's cape. "I don't know about you, but I'm just glad we survived all the way to the denouement," she told her brother as she tied the cape in place around the teddy's neck. It looked just right.

Vernon leaned back and looked at her. "What're you talking about?" he said. "What does that mean?"

"*Denouement?*" his sister replied. "Come on, that's an easy one."

"No, it's not. Just tell me!"

Lisa Marie smiled and gave the King a hug.

"It means," she said, "*the end.*"

THE BATTLE OF TEDDY BEARS CONTINUES!

ABOUT THE AUTHOR

Barry Hutchison was born and raised in the Highlands of Scotland. He was just eight years old when he decided he wanted to become a writer and seventeen when he sold his first piece of work. In addition to the Night of the Living Ted series, he is the author of Invisible Fiends and *The Shark-Headed Bear Thing*. He also writes for TV. Barry lives in Fort William with his partner and their two children.

ABOUT THE ILLUSTRATOR

Lee Cosgrove has been doodling for as long as he can remember. He doodled in his school books and now he is doodling in children's books. He's probably doodling right now while you're reading this! Lee lives with his wife and two children in Cheshire, England.